DEADLY INV...

HUNT FOR EVIL

HAROLD LEA BROWN

DEDICATION

To those who work hard every day to make the Internet and cyberspace a safer place.

ACKNOWLEDGEMENT

Special thanks to Greg Banks for cover artwork, formatting and sage advice in publishing this novel.

CHAPTER 1

KEVIN HASTILY WALKED down the steps of the Gulfstream and ran across the tarmac to the waiting armored van. He turned back to look at the tall man. The door of the van sprung open.

"Jump in, Mr. Albright," Marshal Wes Kindrake said. "You'll be at the Witness Orientation Center in an hour."

Under the cover of night, the armored van rolled to the front gate of a fortified complex. The Witness Protection Safe Site and Orientation Center, (WSSOC) would be Kevin's transition base. A close-circuit camera monitored the driver's every move. He flashed an ID badge to the guard and an electronic gate opened. The van drove into the middle of a courtyard and stopped.

After a moment, Kevin stepped out of the van. He was tired, so tired he felt nothing.

Two uniformed staff met Kevin and escorted him through a set of doors into a heavily secured and controlled environment. It felt more like a prison to keep him in than a facility to keep the bad guys out. Cameras monitored them as they moved down the hall through a series of doors that mysteriously opened and closed as they moved through the complex until they arrived outside of the U.S. Marshal's office. Kevin knew every move had been monitored and someone was verifying who they were before the doors opened and then immediately slammed behind them. With recent incidents of witnesses being killed, they must have stepped up security to protect witnesses—or to cover their asses.

U.S. Marshal Kindrake sat at a desk and flipped through a file, labeled "CASE 12-9652." He took a minute to study Kevin's photo and then closed the file. He leaned back in a well-used wooden tilter chair and closed his eyes for a cat-nap. A knock at the door immediately interrupted his plans.

"Come in," Wes said.

The door opened to reveal Kevin and the two uniformed staff.

"Mr. Albright," Wes said as he stood up to greet Kevin.

Kevin stepped in and stopped to survey the office. He was sweaty, unshaven and just wanted to crash. As badly as he needed a shower, the smell of his t-shirt suggested it needed a cleansing more because of all that his soul had bled into it. All he could think was, *what had he got himself into?* He did not even notice that Wes had extended his hand to greet him.

"Have a seat," Wes said.

As Wes sat back down, Kevin returned to the moment and sat down.

"Kevin. My name's Kevin," he said. He glanced at the file on Wes's desk, "But you already know that."

Wes nodded.

"Right then, Kevin," Wes said, "I think I understand how you are feeling right now."

You don't have a clue how I feel, Kevin thought, *that is unless your pregnant wife has been killed.* But telling this guy how he felt was not going to happen tonight, not ever.

"Where am I?" Kevin said.

"You're at the Witness Protection Safe Site and Orientation Center," Wes said.

"I mean, which city?" Kevin said.

"For reasons of program security, I can't tell you which city you are in, but I can tell you—you are safe."

Kevin appraised Wes with a long slow gaze; the guy almost seemed human, a little different from the other Justice staff he'd met—maybe he could trust him, whatever *trust* meant now. Actually, there was no maybe; Kevin knew he had no choice but to trust him—at least for now.

"That's reassuring, I guess," Kevin said.

"From this moment on you are in the Federal Witness Protection Program," Wes said. "I will be your lifeline to the outside world until Rodriguez Garcia's trial—I will repeat this many times, but it's important that you remember this."

"Now what?" Kevin said. He just wanted to get the basic formalities over with so he could get to his apartment or room—what ever they had set up for him.

"Get you settled in," Wes said. "The important thing tonight is that you get some rest. You'll need it for the work we've got to do in the days ahead."

"Then—" Kevin said. Even though he wanted to get to his new accommodations, he was curious about what lie ahead.

"Tomorrow we start preparations for your new life," Wes replied.

"New life?" Kevin said.

"Yep," Wes said, "Kevin Albright died in a car crash, burned beyond recognition."

"Right," Kevin said as he tried to wrap his mind around what was happening to his life. He'd lost his wife, an unborn son. And now, he was losing his friends, his business, his AA support system and his identity. This was worse than going into rehab; at least in rehab he still had Julia and his true friends.

* * * * *

Wes opened the door to a WSSOC apartment and nodded to Kevin to enter.

Kevin glanced around the apartment. It looked more like a slum motel room from a former life. Just one room—sparsely decorated with second or third hand furniture. *No wonder the blinds were pulled*, he thought.

"I planned to have some of your clothes and personal items for you," Wes said. Then he paused. "Unfortunately everything was destroyed in a fire."

"Fire," Kevin said spinning around.

Kevin hoped the only thing that linked him to Julia was still alive. Sebastian had been out chasing squirrels in the neighborhood that night and was nowhere to be found when he had to make a quick exit. All he was able to grab was a couple of personal possessions.

"I haven't gotten all the details yet," Wes said, "but it appears that someone might have torched your place. Neighbors spotted a suspicious vehicle in the area."

Wes motioned to a cardboard box on the small kitchen table.

Kevin looked at the box label, "JOHNNIE WALKER SCOTCH." He swallowed hard. He could already taste the contents.

Was *God* or the *devil* playing with him, or was it merely coincidence? He had already had too much coincidence in his life. His best friend, Wesley, died in a car accident caused by Wesley's own intoxicated father. Wesley was only eleven years old. Then he was the one who discovered his father's body. Then a drug deal gone wrong in the middle of nowhere killed Julia and their unborn son. His job was zeros and ones, but numbers, a specific number had become the story of his life.

He opened the box. The contents did not match the label. It was a good thing. He was sure that if they had, he would have given in at that very moment.

"They get a license plate?" Kevin asked.

"No, but they got a bit of a description of two men."

"One of them tall? Blond?" Kevin casually asked as he dumped the contents of the box on the table, a golf shirt, two pairs of socks, shorts and a razor.

Wes shook his head he didn't know, but noticed Kevin was staring at the Johnnie Walker box.

"Don't know. That's all the information I have at the moment," Wes said. He started to leave and saw Kevin still staring at the Johnnie Walker box and stopped.

"We'll talk more in the morning. Try to get some sleep."

Kevin looked into Wes's eyes; maybe this was more than just a job for the U.S. Marshal. He hoped that after he got some sleep the feeling he had about Wes would still ring true.

* * * * *

Kevin stroked the whisker stubble on his chin as he cased the room. He froze as he caught a glimpse of a man's image, unshaven, haggard—it looked like his father. His eyes blinked rapidly, like an Etch-a-Sketch machine trying to erase an image. *Who was that man?* He ran his fingers through his hair; then his eyes widened as he realized he was the man in the bathroom mirror.

* * * * *

"Mr. Albright," Wes said, closing a file labeled, "CASE 12-9652." He cleared his throat, "Kevin— you'll need to hand over anything in your possession that links you to your past."

Kevin did not seem to hear Wes; he just stared at the file.

Wes pulled the old rickety desk drawer open and tossed a pen into the tray. He tried to close the drawer it jammed.

The sum total of his entire life was now in a file, that file on the desk, Kevin thought, as he still did not notice Wes.

"Damn it," Wes said.

Kevin snapped back into the moment.

"It's just temporary," Wes said as he motioned to the drawer and the bare office walls. "They make it available for us when we come to town and orient new clients."

Temporary, Kevin thought, everything in life had become just "so temporary."

"OK, Mr. Albright," Wes said.

It was time, Kevin realized, time to hand the sum total of the short life he had lived over to the Marshal. Why was this so difficult? He had already lost everything that meant anything to him. This was really just the last step to affirm it. Besides, he kept reminding himself the end-result was that he was no longer a target and he would be free to pursue Julia's killers.

Kevin slowly pulled his wallet out and stared at it for a moment. Julia had bought it for him—a Christmas present two years ago.

"I guess everything I have is right here. I had hoped to have a bit more time—"

"That's pretty standard once it's a go," Wes said. "Things move quickly."

Kevin opened his wallet, pulled out his driver's license and stared at the picture. He was younger, carefree—but that was in the distant past. He handed the license to Wes and continued to search through his wallet.

"Social Security Card," Kevin said as he handed the card to Wes.

"Credit cards? Birth certificate?" Wes asked.

"Here," Kevin said, pulling out a credit card. He flipped it on the desk. "No birth certificate, I left home rather quickly." He reached back into his wallet and pulled out a photograph. It brought a smile to his face. It was a photograph of Julia, Kevin and Sebastian in a happier moment.

"Photograph?" Wes said.

Kevin nodded.

"I'll need to take that as well," Wes said.

Kevin stared at Wes.

"Anything that links you to your past," Wes said.

Kevin tossed the photograph on the desk in front of Wes. "Bet you've seen hundreds of those in your job," Kevin said.

Wes nodded.

"Anything else, Mr. Albright?"

Kevin looks at his empty ring finger, then shook his head no.

"That's it?" Wes said.

Kevin nodded it was. What else did the Marshal think he had? He tossed his wallet on the desk.

"You can keep the wallet," Wes said.

Suddenly restless, Kevin stood and turned toward the window.

"We're working on your new ID. How's Josh Burke sound?" said Wes.

"Josh?" Kevin said as he spun around to face Wes. *How did they pick that name?* he wondered. *It had to be coincidence.*

Wes nodded yes.

Kevin walked to the window and peered through the blinds into the empty courtyard. He heard Julia's voice, "If we have a boy, let's call him Josh."

"Josh Burke," Wes said the name again. "I'll be saying the name, your name, a lot. Part of the process—you'll eat, sleep and dream about Josh Burke. If you talk in your sleep, by the time we're finished you'll even talk like Josh Burke in your sleep."

"Like I never existed," Kevin said turning to Wes.

"Not quite. Kevin Albright did, but he—" Wes said.

"Died," Kevin said, "burnt beyond recognition."

Wes tossed the family photo into his briefcase.

"I heard people in the courtyard last night," Kevin said, "but I couldn't see them. Does anyone ever go outside during the day?"

"Only in the secure area of the courtyard," Wes replied.

"Now what?" Kevin asked.

"We've already started to create a new past for you," Wes said. "A past you'll need to know inside out. Where you lived, worked, went to school, who your parents were, everything you may be asked once you are relocated."

"Am I—was I married?" Kevin asked.

Wes reflected on the question for a moment.

Kevin could see that Wes knew he was struggling with the loss of a wife and baby.

"We figured it would be a piece of history that was really unnecessary. You are and always have been single," Wes said.

Wes was right, Kevin thought. It would have been very difficult to talk to anyone about a former wife—particularly a dead one, it hit too close to home.

CHAPTER 2

THE SAME GULFSTREAM jet that flew Kevin to the witness safe site taxied down a dimly lit tarmac toward an SUV. He knew it was the same jet as he had reached under the seat during the flight and located the old piece of gum he had placed there. Kevin looked through a Gulfstream window and tried to get his bearings.

"We're just outside Fort Worth," Marshal Wes said. He pointed at a black 2010 Ford Explorer, "That's my ride."

Kevin took a deep breath. This was going to be his home base until the trial. For the first time, he was starting to feel a little exposed. At the safe site, he did not give his security a second thought. Now he was less certain. It all stemmed back to the confidence he had in the Attorney General and the Justice Department. They were having trouble protecting high profile witnesses. He told himself that Julia's killing certainly was not high profile. It was important to him. But to the outside world, it was just a housewife caught in the crossfire of some low life drug dealers.

Wes glanced at his watch, "Should have you to your new apartment in about an hour—hour and a half"

Kevin nodded.

* * * * *

Wes stepped off the Gulfstream and double-checked his holstered gun as he surveyed the tarmac. He motioned to Kevin to follow.

"Sorry," Wes said stopping Kevin as he stepped onto the tarmac, "but it's protocol. I need to remind you again that you're in the Federal Witness Protection Program. I will be your only lifeline to the outside world until the trial."

"What if—" Kevin started to ask.

"No what ifs, for reasons of program and personal security. It has to be this way," Wes said. He motioned Kevin to follow him to his Ford Explorer.

* * * * *

As Wes drove them to Kevin's apartment, Kevin's mind was a thousand miles away—it seemed like a lifetime since he last saw Julia, but the pain in his heart felt like it was this morning. He hoped with his "death", he was now off the radar screen of whomever was pursuing him, at least until he could find Julia's killers. Things had moved so quickly and he needed some time to regroup and think about his next steps.

Wes hit the brakes, honked the horn and then hit the gas as they moved through the aggressive, heavy night traffic.

"We've got you a small apartment," Wes said, "some transportation, it's not a XT Sportster, but it'll get you around." He laid on the horn again, and then hit the brakes hard to avoid a car that cut in front of them.

Kevin snapped back to the moment, looked at Wes and nodded.

"Getting to trial could take a while," Wes said. "Rodriguez Garcia's still in a coma and the search is on for his associates. In the meantime, we figured you'd like to get your head into a different space. Got a job lead—local computer firm's recruiting."

Kevin smiled as he thought, *there's a surprise.* He wondered what role Martelli might have played in this whole process, whether Martelli read any of the reports he and Wayne had sent to the Attorney General. Would he be able to really understand the information provided? Would piece any of the clues provided together?

* * * * *

Kevin pulled a bag out of Wes's car. He glanced at the fifty-seven Chev in the next parking stall. It was rustic, but built to last, just like the apartment building. One thing he noticed was it had the original two-tone paint colors, India Ivory and Colonial Cream—a lighter shade of yellow. He knew that because it was same as the fifty-seven Chev he once had.

"They don't make cars like that any more," Kevin said.

"They're hard to find, that's for sure," Wes said.

* * * * *

Wes stopped at apartment door "422" and waited for Kevin, then unlocked the door. He flipped the key to Kevin, "You're home."

Kevin glanced at the key and then stared at the apartment number, "422." The month and day, he married Julia, the month and day he last laid beside her. Four twenty-two, it was crazy—it was her favorite number: it was her birth date. *Just a coincidence of numbers*, he thought.

* * * * *

As Kevin dropped his bag to the floor, Sebastian sprang out of nowhere and leaped up on him. They fell to the floor.

"Sebastian!" Kevin said, as he looked up at Wes and stroked Sebastian's chin. "How did—"

"Someone found him wandering around," Wes said. "Took him to the pound. No one claimed him. Guess everyone thought he died in the fire—thought it was the least we could do."

Kevin scanned the living room and noticed a computer and printer box.

"Is that really a computer?" he asked.

"You can thank the Attorney General's office for that," Wes said. "They instructed me to make sure that you had it—said that you would need it."

Sebastian dropped a slipper at Kevin's feet.

Kevin toyed with Sebastian, ignoring the slipper. "What?" Kevin asked. He knew what Sebastian was waiting for.

Sebastian stared at the slipper.

Kevin waited a bit longer and then he picked the slipper up. He just held the slipper letting the seconds tick by teasing Sebastian even more. It was not an act of cruelty; it was just the way they played the game.

"Take a few days," Wes said. "Get settled, get to know the city."

Kevin nodded agreement to Wes as Sebastian grabbed the slipper in his hand; "Tug-of-war" was on.

Wes searched his jacket pockets and pulled out a set of keys.

"Here's your car keys," he said as he flipped the keys to Kevin. "It's that fifty-seven Chev you admired in the lot."

Kevin shook his head. He just could not believe it.

"Problem?" Wes said.

"Fate," Kevin said as he looked at Sebastian and then Wes.

"Oh yes, I've been told to let you know your XT was not hacked," Wes said.

It caught Kevin by surprise. Why would he be bringing it up?

"I don't understand all the technical details," Wes said. "But the gist of it is NaviGator said they were not hacked, but they claimed you might have had your wireless Navi-Gator communications intercepted."

"Really?" Kevin said.

"That's what they claimed," Wes replied. "But it was not panning out—then they said it was NaviGator operator error—that the operator had shut down your electronic systems accidentally, and they planned to fire her, but—"

"She disappeared," Kevin said.

Wes nodded yes.

Kevin accepted it could have been an operator error, but with the operator's disappearance, it looked more like a case of a person being paid off to send a NaviGator command to kill the electronics.

Wes continued to search his pockets. He pulled out a business card and handed it to Kevin.

"My business card. Memorize the phone number. Job lead's on the back. Make sure you destroy the card."

Wes started to leave, then held up Kevin's bag.

"I need to take the Glock?"

Kevin was surprised. How could he know that? He thought he had managed to conceal it. He planned to use it when he confronted Julia's killers.

"I'd like to keep it," Kevin said.

"No can do, it's—" Wes said.

"Protocol," Kevin said. "Take it." He would have to find another gun.

Wes opened the bag, then stopped and scratched his head.

"That vehicle the night your house burned down—it was a black SUV."

"What about—" Kevin started to say.

"A blond," Wes said, "and some big dude—that's all I have for now."

Wes pulled the Glock out of Kevin's bag, ejected the clip and stuffed the Glock in his belt behind his back. He adjusted his jacket to conceal it and put the clip in a jacket pocket.

Kevin was grateful that was all he'd pull out of the bag. In all the chaos, he had still managed to keep one very personal item.

* * * * *

An opened computer and printer box sat in the corner of the living room. As soon as Wes left, Kevin set up the computer system. He needed to access critical information to move forward on a plan that was evolving in his head on the fly. Wes made it very clear he was not to contact anyone from his former life, including Wayne. But Kevin had to have the information Albright and Helmes provided to the Attorney General. He would access the electronic vault he had set up to store back up copies of key client briefings in case the Albright and Helmes systems crashed. It was accessible from anywhere in the world, as long as you had a computer and an Internet connection— and knew the password.

The vault was his insurance policy to avoid major embarrassments. Imagine being a computer expert standing in front of the NIPC brass or the President to brief them, but you are unable to access your briefing because the computer system is down. In a moment of insecurity, he had also placed copies of his "tools-of-the-trade" in the vault.

He certainly never imagined using the electronic vault from beyond the grave.

Kevin sat at his computer and navigated through a series of screens. He finally paused to study the screen, "Global

File Storage Last Access 042212; if you are not Kevin Albright please contact security." *If you only knew*, he thought to himself.

* * * * *

Kevin pulled pages off the printer. He studied one page in particular headed "ISP TARGETS FOR FEDERAL SEARCH AND SEIZURE - PREPARED FOR FBI BY ALBRIGHT AND HELMES."

He ran his finger down the page and stopped at one particular company listed. He smiled, as he studied the top target profile for Logic Computer Services. It read, "Logic Computer Services Profile: Specialty-Internet Service Provider, High Debt Ratio, Revenue Assessment-Poor, Financial Viability: Chapter 11 Bankruptcy Protection Filed." It was annotated "New investor pending."

Sebastian trotted into the room with a chewed up slipper.

Kevin flipped Wes's business card over and read the handwritten note "JOB INTERVIEW LOGIC COMPUTER SERVICES."

He looked at Sebastian, "Looks like we got a real job."

Sebastian jumped up, putting his front paws on Kevin's lap and dropped his chewed, soggy slipper on him.

CHAPTER 3

ON THE EDGE of the Fort Worth Business District, Kevin located the single story building whose sole occupant was Logic Computer Services. He did not mind the distance he had to drive from his apartment as it gave him a chance to get behind the wheel of a fifty-seven Chev. As he approached the glass doors embossed with "LOGIC COMPUTER SERVICES," Paul Gillis greeted him. Kevin noticed Paul's wrinkled white shirt and loosened tie. It looked like Paul had lived in it for days and the dark circles under his eyes suggested he had slept little in weeks.

"Mr. Burke, I'm Paul Gillis, Operations Manager, here at LCS."

* * * * *

"**K**endell Systems," Paul said flipping through Kevin's resume. "They were very impressed, Mr. Burke, and highly recommended we consider you for employment."

"Yeah, highly classified work," Kevin said. He remembered Wes telling him people would dig into his work history and laying down a past employment history trail could be challenging. One effective cover often used in the witness protection program was to tell a prospective employer the work you did was highly classified—hence, they would not be able to get a lot of detail.

"So I discovered," Paul said. "We weren't able to get a lot of information." Paul set the resume aside, "But the local police department sure processed your security check quickly."

Kevin squirmed a bit, stepping into his new identity was more difficult than he expected.

"That's good, right?" Kevin said.

"You bet," Paul replied. "ISPs are all about confidentiality—but guess I don't have to tell you that."

Kevin nodded in agreement. He did not want to appear to be too smart or over qualified for the job he desperately needed. Paul was right, but he thought that *Paul knew more than he was prepared to share. Maybe he was being played to glean more information.*

"You'll fit in well here," Paul replied.

* * * * *

As Kevin followed Paul on a quick tour of LCS's facility, he was both impressed and puzzled. The offices were a maze of screens and open workspaces at the front of the building, inside a larger area—a room within a room. Instead of an office area bordered by bright exterior windows, the border was a wall made of cement blocks. The blocks created a ten-foot buffer between the building's exterior windows and the office space. Paul said it helped keep the air conditioning costs down. In Kevin's mind, it also kept nosey people at a distance.

The data center was at the rear of the building sitting on a raised floor. Floor tiles elevated above the cement floor provided access to cabling and power for quick set up or dismantling of file servers. The new financial backer had heavily invested in equipment, installing new file servers and backup power capability, to minimize outages. However, the new investor did not want to invest in upgrades to the building's fire suppression system. The fire suppression system was very dated. In fact, newer fire regulations would not allow such an installation, but LCS's system was grandfathered in under old fire regulations. Most operators of data centers and their clients would insist on an effective fire suppression system. Kevin was sure this was a further sign of the slippery slope LCS was on trying to survive and serve a *niche* type of clientele—criminals.

Fire requires oxygen, heat and a source of fuel source to burn. Newer systems attack all three ingredients to suppress a fire. LCS's system used halon gas and worked on the principle of cutting off the oxygen supply in an "air-tight" room in order to suppress a fire.

Kevin knew that once the halon system alarms were triggered, anyone in the data center had less then thirty seconds to evacuate the center or they would die by suffocation. This posed many challenges and was a primary reason halon gas systems were phasing out—too many data center personnel were killed trying to save the data center.

While he tried not to let his mind wander too far ahead, he could not help but think that should LCS investors need to make a quick exit, the suppression system would be one way to take care of LCS staff who perhaps knew too much. However, if the system did its job, all the data on the server's would be preserved. Why would they want to leave this evidence behind? He needed to find out what kind of data was being stored on these file servers.

* * * * *

Kevin exited the LCS office building—upbeat. He had managed to secure a job with LCS. The U.S. Marshal's Service had done a good job creating his employment history. He had almost slipped up once and referred to Albright and Helmes, but quickly caught himself.

He needed to keep playing the name Josh Burke over and over in his head, to make sure he did not let the name Kevin Albright slip into any conversation. Every time he heard his name—Josh—referred to, he thought of Julia and their unborn son. He gave his head a shake—too much thinking. He started to walk briskly, weaving in and out of pedestrians. He studied the street signs and buildings, a diversion to take his mind off Julia. Besides he wanted to become very familiar with his new surroundings.

* * * * *

Kevin tossed and turned on an uncomfortable couch in his apartment living room. He had not slept in a bed since the day before his tenth wedding anniversary. The last time he was even in a bed, it was the guestroom at Wayne's, when he and Julia slipped out of the anniversary party and had made love. In all honesty, they didn't make love. They had sex. They did not have time to make love; it was just lust, sweat, sweet and quick. Now, he became overwhelmed with thoughts of Julia almost as soon as he tried to crawl into a bed.

Kevin opened his eyes and glanced around the room. Where was he? He looked at his hands. He was holding the blood-stained white shirt. He glanced at the coffee table—covered with articles and printouts. Right, he was at the apartment. Then he realized the television was blaring. He searched through all the paper on the coffee table for the remote, but could not find it. He checked his watch; it was barely nine in the evening. He turned on the couch to face inward and pulled a blanket over his head. If he hoped to be effective at getting Julia's killer, or keeping the new job, he needed to get at least a few hours sleep.

* * * * *

Kevin was in a business suit worn like wrinkled polyester. He staggered down a dark seedy alley, and then stopped to steady himself. He forced a bottle to his mouth, took a swig, and paused to read the label, "Johnnie Walker Blue." It didn't matter; he couldn't taste anything but alcohol, the magic ingredient that numbed the pain. He would never make it to the next anniversary. There would never be a family, unless he ended it forever.

A paunchy man lurched out the shadows and grabbed for his bottle.

Kevin pushed him away. Then, he carefully set the bottle down.

The paunchy man regained his balance and pulled out a blade.

Kevin defended his *Fort Knox*—he charged and delivered a series of blows.

The paunchy man swung the blade wildly and caught Kevin on the cheek.

The pain ignited Kevin; he delivered a punch that sent the paunchy man to the pavement. Then Kevin whipped out a Glock 37 and pointed it at the paunchy man. He put his finger on the trigger, started to squeeze it, then stopped—a moment of sanity. He stuffed it back into his polyester slacks. He moved closer to the paunchy man. The sweat poured off him. He reached down and picked up the blade beside the man who had tried to kill him for his Johnnie Walker Blue scotch and tossed it into the garbage dumpster.

In the shadows, Kevin straightened his tie, then picked up his Johnnie Walker Blue and guzzled it. Before he could finish the contents, he crashed into the side of the dumpster, bounced off a brick wall and dropped to the pavement. Bleeding, he tightly clutched the bottle.

* * * * *

Kevin's eyes snapped open as he heard a Johnnie Walker liquor commercial blast out from the television. He was in a cold sweat and disoriented. He sat up and zeroed in on the closet. *It would be so easy,* he thought. He could just bury all this pain.

Sebastian came bounding into the room.

Kevin glanced at him and sprang to his feet; he knew what he had to do.

* * * * *

The room was filled with smoke, worn out furniture and people who greeted each other with hugs, smiles and laughter.

Kevin entered the AA meeting room—the room was familiar. All over the world, twenty-four hours a day, there were AA meetings going on. Fort Worth was no different, and he had located a group that held meetings at three in the morning.

An AA member spotted Kevin and immediately approached him.

He could not help but notice her T-Shirt slogan, "Scotch Free."

"You look like you need a hug," she said.

Before he had a chance to think about it, she hugged him.

"Tough night, huh?" She said.

"Aren't they all?" Kevin said.

"You're in the right place," she said. "Grab a coffee and meet the gang."

Kevin knew he was in the right place. He had lost his support systems, his anchors. And if he was ever going to stand a chance of getting Julia's killers, he needed this place, at least for now. Keeping some sense of sanity depended on it.

* * * * *

Kevin took a sip of his black coffee as he pretended to listen to an AA member beside him, but the voices in his head seemed to be winning.

Then he heard the woman who introduced herself when he arrived, "Everyone fill your coffees and a seat—we'll start in two minutes."

Kevin glanced at the coffeepot and watched a line quickly form. Then something caught his attention. It was the backside profile of a woman at the front of the line. She was pouring a coffee. He did a double take. Even her over-sized hoodie and jeans could not hide the resemblance to Julia.

The woman turned to catch Kevin's eyes fixed on her.

Kevin immediately looked at the floor. He could not believe his eyes. She was early thirties. Her features mirrored Julia's in so many ways. Even the same premature crow's-feet framed her blue eyes.

He looked up and noticed she was talking to an AA member. Then he heard her laugh and she looked his way. She flashed him a friendly smile and walked toward him. His eyes followed her, as he felt his heart start to race.

She walked past him and took a seat at the back of the room.

* * * * *

Joe ripped his tie off and threw it on the office credenza. It landed beside a picture of Joe, the Attorney General and

Secretary of State. All these late nights with no payoff were starting to take their toll on him. He did not have a personal life. His life was his job. But if something didn't break soon, he could kiss a job in politics goodbye. Then he wouldn't even have a life. His phone rang. He looked at the call display—it was U.S. Marshal Wes Kindrake. He snapped up the phone.

"Good news, I hope," Joe said without wasting anytime.

"He's in at Logic Computer Services," Wes said.

Joe leaned back in his chair. It was the news he really needed to hear. *His plan was working*, he thought to himself. He hung up the phone, and looked at an open red folder. The report, "ISP TARGETS FOR FEDERAL SEARCH AND SEIZURE - PREPARED FOR FBI BY ALBRIGHT AND HELMES," stared back at him. He smiled to himself, closed the folder and dropped it into the shredder.

CHAPTER 4

KEVIN WALKED THROUGH the main doors of Logic Computer Services. It was nearing midnight as he watched Paul slam down the telephone at the reception desk. LCS had filed for bankruptcy protection and Kevin suspected the stress to turn things around was getting to Paul.

Paul caught Kevin out of the corner of his eye as he entered. At once, he smiled and approached him.

"Hi, Josh," Paul said, as he gave Kevin a friendly slap on the back. "I really appreciate you taking the night shift—workload has skyrocketed recently."

He wasn't fooling Kevin. Kevin knew the smile and act were forced, but he played along.

"Not sleeping much at nights anyway," he said. Which was true, *but if Paul only knew why*, he thought. "So what's the deal?" Kevin asked. "New clients?"

"Yeah, new clients, new accounts and lots of traffic," Paul said.

"Local or international?" Kevin responded. He noticed Paul's raised eyebrows. *Damn it,* he thought. *Slow down, Albright,* he said to himself. *It's your first night.*

"Come on Josh," Paul said, "Let's meet the team and get you on a workstation."

Kevin followed Paul as he navigated the partitioned maze to a corner cubicle.

Paul stopped and rapped on the top of the screen's wooden edging as if entering an enclosed office.

"Meet your new neighbor, Josh Burke," he said to the cubicle occupant.

Meg swiveled around.

Kevin froze as he thought, *You, the woman from the AA meeting.* Only now, she wore a business pants suit.

"Josh meet Megan Taylor," Paul said introducing them.

Meg politely smiled and stood.

"Ms. Taylor's a recent recruit too." Paul said.

Kevin was mesmerized—transported to another time, as he stared at Meg.

She extended her hand, and Kevin's fixation on her created an awkward moment for Meg. Uncomfortable, she glanced at the tops of her shoes.

Kevin still did not respond.

"Nice to meet you, Mr. Burke. Call me, Meg."

Paul's smartphone rang and Kevin snapped back into the moment, embarrassed he had ignored Meg's extended hand. He immediately gripped her hand and shook it hard, as if he wanted her to know they were just going to be colleagues—nothing more.

"Josh is going to be working the night shift for a while," Paul said, as he looked at his smartphone display. The caller was "International Antiques."

Kevin noticed Paul's eyes widen.

Paul immediately turned in attention back to Kevin, "I've got to run," he said as he pointed at the next cubicle. "Make yourself at home."

Kevin watched Paul rush down the aisle, and then he entered his new temporary workspace—a cubicle. It was a far cry from the plush private office he once enjoyed and owned at Albright and Helmes. In a way, he felt he needed this. He needed to be punished, to suffer—it was a way to pay for the guilt he felt.

Meg poked her head over cubicle screen and said, "Maybe—"

Kevin jumped back.

"Sorry, didn't mean to startle you," she said. "I was just going to say maybe we could go for coffee sometime."

Paul's office door slammed.

Kevin looked down the aisle at Paul's office. He was engaged in a very heated telephone conversation.

After a moment, he had seen enough and turned to Meg, "Coffee would be fine."

* * * * *

Kevin studied a computer printout titled "INTERNET TRAFFIC LOG - NIGHT OPS." He ran his finger across the column headings "CLIENT, COUNTRY OF ORIGIN, RUN PROCEDURE."

Multitasking, he glanced up at his computer screen. It flashed, "Internet Traffic Log Monitoring."

Paul appeared out of nowhere.

"Problem?" he asked.

Shit, Kevin thought to himself as he dropped the printout. He searched for an excuse—a reason to hide his surprise.

"Trying to learn all I can about the job," he said. What a lame answer, he fought even harder to hide his surprise, "I thought you went home." He should have stopped; he was only digging a deeper hole.

"Just run the traffic log procedure," Paul said as he glared at Kevin. "When prompted—delete the damn file."

Kevin nodded. He needed to be more careful, and he needed to dial back his eagerness to dig into what was happening at LCS. Otherwise, he suspected they would fire him before he could find the clues he needed to figure out if, and how, Internet Service Providers factored into the men who killed Julia.

* * * * *

Meg had discovered a small quaint restaurant down the block from LCS. LCS employees rarely went there as it catered to a family crowd. No smoking was allowed and more importantly, no alcohol was served. Kevin and Meg had agreed to meet there at the end of their night shift.

As the waitress walked away from a quiet corner table, it suddenly became an awkward moment for Kevin, and he hoped Meg felt the same. Kevin tried not to stare at Meg. Other than Wes, he was lucky to talk to another human being, a kindred AA spirit to boot. But as soon as he was sitting across the table from Meg, he questioned why he had really agreed to meet Meg. Maybe playing the slipper game with Sebastian was all he was really ready for.

"So what do you think about LCS?" Meg said.

After a moment Kevin realized Meg had spoken, "I'm sorry, it's just—you remind me so much of someone." He tried to refocus, to get his mind off thoughts about how much Meg resembled Julia. "LCS, well," Kevin said, "Paul seems to be under the gun."

"They're going through a tough financial stretch," Meg quickly said.

Kevin was surprised she knew this—she had just started. She was just a "lowly non-management" employee like he was.

"Really?" he said. "But they seem to be so busy." He thought, *maybe Meg could provide some INTEL on LCS, something he could use to find out who had stepped in to control LCS.*

Meg stirred her coffee in silence.

"Do you know who their clients are?" Kevin said.

"Not really," she looked up at Kevin. "Why?"

"You can learn a lot about a computer company by the clients they have," Kevin said as he fought the need to ask her what she really knew. He remembered how being overly eager nearly created a problem with Paul. Maybe she was spying on him for Paul, a sort of company safe guard check on new hires.

Meg sipped her coffee and then asked, "Learned anything yet?"

Kevin had a sudden guilt attack. He felt like he was cheating on Julia. He was just having coffee with an office colleague who was also trying to stay sober. He tried to convince himself it was a good thing. He looked into Meg's eyes. He instantly turned away. Why did he do that, look into her eyes? He tried to refocus on watching her sip her coffee. His eyes drifted back to Meg's eyes—like a compass to magnetic north. It was not working. He felt even guiltier when she smiled at him. He needed to get out of there.

"Listen, I've got to go," he said glancing at his watch. He jumped up from the table.

"What are you doing Saturday?" she asked.

Kevin knew the only thing he was doing was walking Sebastian. He needed an excuse.

"Might be getting in some overtime," he replied.

"It's July 4th!" Meg said.

"My AA birthday," Kevin blurted out.

"We could celebrate it," Meg said.

Damn it, he thought. He had stepped into that one, but he did not respond.

CHAPTER 5

KEVIN HATED SPENDING time in his apartment at night. The nights were long without Julia beside him. Getting Julia's killers fully consumed him. It was why he did not mind the night shift at LCS and it might have explained why he was so diligent at his desk. His unusual upbeat demeanor on the night shift had opened him up to ribbing from many of his colleagues, with one notable exception—Meg, as they would rather be at home sleeping or doing anything else but sitting in front of a computer screen.

He thought he had figured out Meg's reason for the night shift. Recovering alcoholics don't sleep much. They wander around their empty places, go to AA meetings, work or—resort to drinking.

Paul had begun squeezing everyone to work more hours for less pay to avoid the ultimate outcome, bankruptcy. It definitely was not a great motivator to the group of professionals working at LCS. The number of call-ins for sick days or nights was increasing, but that was good for Kevin. He got to work seven nights a week. Paul was beginning to worship him and Meg for their dedication—another reason they ribbed him—he was sucking up to the boss and was putting the moves on the new gal.

Tonight, he was totally absorbed, studying a printout and periodically checking his computer screen to gauge the

status of a program he was running. It was a search and destroy program. The program aggregated traffic that had
moved through LCS in a twenty-four hour period, and
flagged it for destruction. At that moment, the screen
flashed, "TRAFFIC LOG RUN PROCEDURE," and then
a computer prompt flashed "CHOOSE DELETE."

Kevin turned back to the computer printout; his finger
moved down the listing and stopped at "COUNTRY OF
ORIGIN IRAQ"—then traced across to "RUN
PROCEDURE DELETE" and "CLIENT
INTERNATIONAL ANTIQUES." Kevin's curiosity was
peaked. Their traffic volume was growing. Anything involving Iraq, North Korea or China sent up more red flags for
him and reference to International Antiques just added to
the mystery. He tapped his finger beside the client company
name International Antiques.

Meg poked her head over the screen, "So?"

Kevin nearly jumped out of his skin.

"Next time," Meg said as she rapped on the wooden
screen top, "I'll knock."

"I'm running against a deadline," Kevin said as he held
up a printout.

"Give Saturday any more thought?" Meg asked.

Kevin glanced at his computer.

"Josh, it's just a little picnic in the park," Meg said.

Kevin just wanted to get this procedure run and off his
desk before the end of the shift; he needed to find out who
was behind LCS's growth in traffic. He certainly did not
want Paul to be on his case about a failure to destroy traffic
logs.

He glanced up at Meg. Her blue eyes penetrated the brick wall to his sensibilities, just like Julia always seemed to do. He needed to get back to work. He had to get this information; it was for Jewels.

He caved and nodded yes, he was on for it. It would be a necessary distraction, he told himself, an opportunity to pump Meg for more information about LCS activities. He was still not certain he could trust Meg enough to share any significant INTEL he had gathered. But, on the other hand, she might have INTEL he could use.

* * * * *

Big D was feeling good, really good, as he strolled down the hall to the International Antiques hacker's office. He had consumed a couple of cognacs and smoked two Cuban cigars. He hoped they were about to do what everyone kept saying was impossible, hack into the world's largest intergovernmental cooperation law enforcement agency, INTERPOL.

It was not the first time, or the second time. It had become pretty much a routine. INTERPOL would suspect their information had been compromised. They would redouble their efforts to strengthen their computer security. That would temporarily halt Big D's access to their database and information. In the end, he always relished the moment Hazze *beat* the new security installed and he was operational again. Like other organizations Big D had penetrated, INTERPOL had never really determined if they had been hacked into. They only had suspicions. That was the beauty of the whole thing—they were invisible or as he like to call them, *secret agents.*

Big D entered Hazze's office and said tongue in cheek, "Crack INTERPOL's new impenetrable security system yet?"

"Our guy's working on the last fix at his end," Hazze said. "I've got one program tweak at my end and then we'll be back in business."

"I'm gonna need an information swap," Big D said. "You know—fingerprints, dentals, photos, the full deal."

"Got the names you want to swap?" Hazze said, rubbing his hands together.

"Soon, very soon," Big D said. He turned and walked toward the door.

"D," Hazze said, "my colleague says thanks."

Big D smiled to himself. He expected as much and kept walking, his back to Hazze. He gave Hazze a thumbs-up over his shoulder as he walked out the door.

* * * * *

Kevin sat on his apartment couch and studied a telephone directory printout. He paused for a moment and glanced around the sparsely decorated living room. For the first time, he noticed how badly stained the couch was. *It wasn't a place Jewels would like,* he thought. Then he heard her giggle. *Who was he kidding? She loved everyone and everything*—he was the problem.

He turned his attention back to the telephone directory and ran his finger down the page, past more than two dozen names—all with the last name "SPITZ." *There's got to be something here*, he thought. But whatever it was, it just was not resonating with him at the moment. He had called every Spitz number listed in the telephone directory without success. No one had anything to do with, or knowledge of, the Spitz murder, except what they may have read in the newspaper.

He glanced over at his computer screen; it displayed the United States Government Company's Registry website, "Searching for International Antiques." Kevin's mind was in overdrive again. *What the hell was he really doing?* he wondered. *Was this really about getting his wife's killers? Or was he a coward staying busy to avoid killing himself with booze? Or was he just like everyone else—fearful of losing a spouse? Afraid that something he would do would cross the line and he would remember it? Or all of the above?* Maybe he really did have a death wish, only in reverse of Charles Bronson. He was recklessly pursuing professional killers, hoping *they* whoever *they* were, would just kill him and put him out of his misery, before he started drinking again. Maybe he was in shock after Julia's death and acting prematurely.

Drinking would be far worse than dying. Drinking would be a betrayal of everything that Jewels had sacrificed to support him gaining sobriety. Wayne was right. He was out of his league. But he made a promise to Jewels—he actually made two promises to Jewels. The first was not to drink. And the second was to get the thug that killed her. He intended to keep both.

His computer beeped. *At last, maybe a clue*, he hoped. He bounced off the couch and was at his computer in five steps. He plunked down in front of the monitor and read the display, "No record found." He sat back in his chair.

He was not used to running into dead ends—hitting the proverbial wall like this. In his former life, he would bounce from clue to clue, each clue getting him closer to his objective until he zeroed in on the culprit.

He keyed another search request into his computer. The screen flashed, "Motor Vehicle Database Searching SUV Records." Kevin knew the search could take a while, so he grabbed the newspaper that sat nearby. He unfolded it and flipped through the pages, as if he was only looking at the pictures. Then one headline smacked him in the face, "WOMAN INNOCENT VICTIM OF DRUG DEAL GONE BAD."

Now that he was "dead" and in witness protection, information about that terrible night was leaking out through the cracks. *Two things that were bad about this,* he thought. *They killed Julia and he was still alive.*

As he scanned down the page, he saw another headline, "ATTORNEY GENERAL BELIEVES REVIEW WILL PROVE ANONYMITY NOT COMPROMISED."

Kevin was sure Joe Martelli knew someone at the paper, or the paper had ties to the Attorney General somehow, as coincidently, the article was in a smaller type font and buried. Unlike everyone else in the witness protection program, where the criminals knew their informant was alive, but hidden, Kevin was dead—at least that is what he hoped those after him still believed.

He slumped back in his chair. There was silence. He hated these moments—it was as if he and everyone around him had died, and he was somehow able to watch and hear it—death.

Sebastian's nails clicked on the linoleum floor as he approached Kevin brought him back to the moment—to life. Sebastian dropped his wet nose on Kevin's lap. Sebastian was the last link to Julia. She had picked out Sebastian at a dog shelter—abandoned and undernourished. He cowered whenever a human approached him. He had thought about that many times over the years as in many ways Sebastian mirrored the man he was back then. He felt alone in a crowd, abandoned by his father and insecure—then rescued. Most of his wardrobe did not fit and his hair was falling out, the result of binge drinking and not eating properly.

Sebastian was the first step on Kevin's journey to sobriety and a family Julia wanted. Julia did not judge him. She loved him unconditionally. He wanted to realize her dreams too, but he knew sobriety was the biggest hurtle to having a baby and it would take actions and time, not words.

All his life, people had told him *how* he should feel. And his father told him what he would be—a failure, a drunk and all alone, just like he was when he died. However, AA taught him that no one could tell him what he really felt. He had to experience, decide and deal with his feelings without alcohol to stay sober.

He knew Sebastian missed Julia too, as he stroked his chin, something Julia often did. And just as Sebastian did when Julia stroked his chin, Sebastian drooled.

Kevin's computer beeped. He glanced up as the computer screen flashed, "Access Denied."

"Damn it," Kevin snarled as he pushed a pile of computer printouts to the floor and leaped to his feet. He quickly sat down after he realized he had sent Sebastian scrambling across the living room floor.

"Sorry buddy, I didn't mean to take it out on you," Kevin said. He called Sebastian back, stroked his chin and surveyed the mess he had just created. *Well, Jewels*, he thought, *you always told me to clean up my messy papers. I hope you are getting a good laugh out of this.*

* * * * *

As Kevin organized the last of the computer printouts on his apartment computer desk, he thought about his next steps. If he were back at Albright and Helmes, he would just hack into the vehicle database to show the client their security needed to be improved. Of course, they would have been under contract to attempt the break in, but you can't contract a dead man, he told himself.

Kevin turned to his computer. As he accessed his hacking tools stored in the electronic vault, he tried to rationalize his next actions. A few screens and keystrokes later, Kevin entered his password into his Global File Account. The screen flashed back, "Kevin Albright Account Closed-Client Deceased." His Global File Account had been closed. To add insult, he was able to use his password to gain access to this screen. He should have known this was coming and moved everything from the electronic vault to a new vault.

He needed his hacking tools. The only recourse was his former company, Albright and Helmes. Kevin prayed that because he had died, there would not have been a sense of urgency for Wayne to deactivate his account or password.

Kevin moved through a series of computer screens and arrived at his Albright and Helmes account login screen. He breathed a sigh of relief—his account still existed. The next step was to enter his password. He took a deep breath. He keyed in his password. The screen flashed back, "Welcome Back, Kevin Albright". Kevin inhaled; he was in.

Sebastian approached Kevin, as if sensing the relief.

Kevin grabbed Sebastian's front paws and they did a happy dance, as if he had reconnected with a long lost friend.

* * * * *

Kevin's eyes were trained on the monitor in his living room. He never thought he would be hacking into a government database as a private citizen. It was just like his early days as an alcoholic. He rationalized and bargained with himself, if I drink today, I won't drink tomorrow. However, this time he rationalized to himself, if I hack into the government database, I am really helping the government with business—finding Julia's killers.

At some point, he would alert the government to the holes in computer security for the government systems he had hacked. But they were not playing ball with him and at the moment, he would reserve timing of a decision to play ball with them.

He looked at his computer screen, "HackPack Installed, Motor Vehicle Database Searching SUV Records." He had become one of them, a hacker, breaking into secure databases to steal information. However, he had little time to think about what he had just done, as the computer screen started processing his request.

Within seconds, it flashed up a list of vehicles cross-referenced by type and driver's license. It was too late to fight against any sort of temptation; the government information was already stolen and displayed on his computer. He looked at the screen and studied the column headings, "Black SUVs Eastern States by License Number, Owner, Hair Color, Height." Then, he ran his finger down the Hair Color Column, right past the license plate number "6T0 9W5, Carlos Steelie, Hair Color Brown."

Kevin shook his head in disbelief. *How could that be?* He turned to Sebastian. He was chewing on a shredded slipper. As if Sebastian was human, Kevin said to him, "Who are we kidding here Albright? He wouldn't register it—he's not alive!"

* * * * *

Kevin stood in his office cubicle and surveyed the office floor for activity. The night shift was usually quieter, but Paul was in most nights and his moods were becoming fouler. Everyone kept their heads down and did their jobs— the alternative was death by firing.

Unfortunately, the economy did not afford the high-techs once in short supply the luxury choice of walking away. At the moment, Paul's office was empty. Meg was in tonight as well, but was not at her desk. This was perfect.

Kevin did not need anyone walking in on him while he was gathering information about one of Logic Computer Services' clients.

He pulled a chair up to his computer and his fingers jumped on the keys. A series of cryptic commands flashed across the monitor and the computer shifted into turbo-drive. Soon, the computer screen was flashing, "Capturing International Antique Traffic." He was trapping every email and text message received, stored or sent by or to an International Antique client in the past twenty-four hours. Kevin would be able to study them later.

This was the beauty and the bane of new age communications. Traditional telephone calls were never recorded—unless there was a wiretap or the party left a message in a voice mailbox. There was a record of who called, who was called and the time of the call. However, every text message and email was a digital communication, automatically captured by the Telco, in addition to details about the sender and the receiver.

* * * * *

Meanwhile, Paul was preoccupied as he walked onto the floor and strolled directly to his office. He closed his office door and grabbed the phone.

* * * * *

Kevin's monitor flashed, "Microdecrypt Installed. File Decrypting." The Internet traffic was encrypted and unreadable. The software used by Kevin turned each piece of email downloaded into something that could be read by his computer. He needed to re-encrypt it with encryption software he had designed and transfer it to his high-density flash drive. He would be the only person who could read it, should Paul accidentally get his hands on the high-density flash drive. Nervous, Kevin stood and clasped his hands behind his head as he stared at his computer.

As Paul waited for his call to be completed, he turned to survey the floor. He spotted Kevin standing at his desk.

Kevin's monitor flashed, "Reading International Antiques Traffic." Kevin glanced up just as Paul turned away. It looked like Paul was in another very heated phone conversation. *This seemed to be almost turning into a nightly ritual.* This was good for Kevin, as Paul would be on the phone for a while. Kevin turned back to his computer. The screen flashed, "Encrypting Traffic with Kalbright."

Paul hung up and noticed Kevin was still standing at his desk.

Kevin's eyes were glued to his monitor as if that would speed up the process. The screen flashed, "Copying International Antiques Traffic to USB flash drive."

Paul walked out of his office and started down the aisle toward Kevin.

* * * * *

Meg had quietly returned to her desk and watched Kevin. His eyes were glued to his monitor. He obviously did not realize she was back at her desk.

She thought about telling him she was back, but she did not want to appear clingy. He looked so intense and she did not want to give him another one of those "heart attack" moments where he jumped through the ceiling.

* * * * *

Kevin's monitor flashed, "Copying International Antiques Traffic Files." Finally, he was doing the job he was paid to do, almost. He would delete the traffic files as soon as copying to the USB drive was completed.

Once the files were deleted, if the FBI raided LCS, there would be no traffic history in their server to seize, as the last step each night was to scrub the servers. Now he was on the inside and he understood the key steps performed to prevent the FBI from getting critical information on ISP targets he had flagged for their raids.

He wiped the sweat running down his cheeks. Tonight, it was taking longer than he remembered to run this type of computer procedure.

* * * * *

Moments later, Meg rushed into the aisle, stumbled and clumsily dropped a pile of printouts on the floor right in Paul's path.

* * * * *

Kevin's computer screen flashed, "Copying International Traffic Files Completed."

He pulled his chair close to the monitor. His fingers jumped on the keys, a rapid series of clicks followed and his computer screen flashed, "Deleting Traffic Files."

* * * * *

Paul stopped in the aisle to help Meg pick up the printouts. Meg hoped her move had been enough to stall Paul from seeing what Kevin was up too.

* * * * *

Kevin yanked the USB flash drive from computer and stuffed it into his pocket, and whipped around in his chair to see who his visitor was.

Meg entered his workspace cubicle and pushed a pile of printouts into his face.

"Josh, here are your printouts,' she said.

Paul was right behind Meg. He stopped and stared at Meg and Kevin. He gave everything in Kevin's cubicle the once over glance and then looked at Kevin's computer monitor. It was flashing "All Traffic Files Deleted." Satisfied, he proceeded down the hall.

Not sure what Meg had seen, Kevin looked at the printouts. They were all blank paper.

"Thanks, Meg."

"Just trying to help," Meg replied.

Kevin watched Meg walk away and turned to his computer screen to see what Paul might have seen. It was flashing "All Traffic Files Deleted." He took a deep breath; he knew that he was cutting things close, too close. Tonight, Paul would have caught him, if it had not been for Meg's help.

CHAPTER 6

K EVIN RUSHED INTO his apartment living room—he had just finished his night shift. He did not even notice he had run by his best friend, Sebastian, who had waited all night for him to come home. He jammed the USB flash drive into his computer.

Moments later, Kevin impatiently watched the cursor pulse. He punched the ENTER key several times. He of all people, a techie, should have known that this was not going to speed up processing of his request for information by a computer. But in the techie world, impatience—waiting for a computer response, was universally passed through fingertips to the ENTER key to the computer with each tap. It was programmed with zeros and ones—numbers that turned people into faceless things dealt with inhumanly. Requests that were cued up and dealt with one at a time, based on the parameters submitted.

It was not a face-to-face customer service encounter. A highly technical impersonal relationship between techies and their computers had become mainstream for the next generation. Kids didn't even use the telephone anymore to talk to someone. They elected to send impersonal text messages. *Five steps forward, from the impersonal days of Morse code to the telephone, four steps backward to texting,* he thought. His mind was wondering again as he waited for the computer to action his request.

Finally, the computer responded splashing out a list of names, addresses and employers across the screen. He ran his finger down the list. Where were the names he suspected, like SPITZ? His finger ran past "Donald Wilson Deceased, Brent Tengler, Jack."

The phone rang. He jumped, nearly launching into orbit. "Jesus, Kevin, Lighten up," he said to himself. It rang again. He took a deep breath and picked up the phone receiver.

"Josh. It's Wes."

Finally, some news, Kevin thought.

* * * * *

Joe paced Wes's small office, as he listened to the conversation on Wes's speakerphone.

"They get him?" Kevin said.

"Attorney General's office has run," Wes glanced up to see Joe shake his head no. "They're running leads on the blond suspect—Colombia's still in a coma."

"Colombia?" Kevin said.

"Sorry, Rodriguez Garcia—one of his aliases is Colombia," Wes said.

* * * * *

"I'm going home," Kevin said as he shook his head in disgust. "I'll get her killers." He wanted to hang the phone up, but he hoped he could get some information—anything to help him.

* * * * *

Joe grabbed Wes by the arm and mouthed, "No fucking way."

Wes yanked his arm from Joe's grip, and said, "You go home, the case goes on the back burner."

"What the—" Kevin said.

"We've got thousands of people in protection playing by the rules," Wes said. "You quit, we'll have to," he paused to allow Kevin to fill in the blank.

* * * * *

Kevin waited for Wes to finish the sentence. He did not. Kevin contemplated his next steps. No solutions were coming to mind at the moment. One thing he knew for sure was he needed witness protection until he had a better plan.

"So now what?" he was forced to ask,

* * * * *

Joe signaled Wes to pump Kevin for information.

"Things OK with the new job?" Wes asked.

"What?" Kevin said.

"Well," Wes paused then said, "given your background, just wondered if you're putting your skills to good use—using that computer provided."

He caught Joe's scowl out of the corner of his eye.

* * * * *

Kevin held the phone receiver away from his ear and looked at it in total disbelief.

"Hello, Josh," Wes said.

Kevin put the receiver back to his ear.

"Is there anything that you want me to relay to the Attorney General?" Wes asked.

Kevin slammed the receiver down.

* * * * *

A CIA agent skated across the lobby floor of the Central Intelligence Agency headquarters building. It was as slippery as ice, and the CIA's shield and mission "We are the nation's first line of defense. We accomplish and go where others cannot go," marked center ice. He had a folder tucked under his arm and jumped into a waiting elevator and went straight to the top floor, where the CIA's top decision-makers worked.

* * * * *

A quick knock and the agent entered the CIA Director's office.

The CIA Director spun around and slammed the phone down on his mahogany desk, "Do we know where all that computer traffic is originating?" he asked.

"Our Iraqi INTEL sourced inbound traffic as being routed through Russia and possibly North Korea," the agent said, tossing the file on the desk.

"Can we decrypt the damn stuff yet?" the CIA Director asked.

The agent shook his head no.

"Chatter about a plot to curtail oil and gas exports to the U.S. is picking up," the agent said.

The Director sat back in his chair. "And," he said, prompting the agent to continue.

"Not sure if it's just OPEC members saber rattling," the agent said, "or whether we've got some rogue oil producing country signaling they want something more for their oil."

"Turn the heat up on our Iraqi operatives," the Director said. "Tell them we need sources verified and the damn decryption code, if they want the Security Council to keep *their* funds flowing."

"Right away, Director," the agent said.

The Director's phone rang. He looked at the caller ID display; it was the "Chair, National Security Council." He glanced at the agent and motioned him to leave and get on with the orders he had just dispatched.

CHAPTER 7

There were pockets of people everywhere in the park, all staking out their picnic tables and favorite treed spots for shelter from a hot sun, and all celebrating July 4. The hot sun seemed to turn many of them into *temporary* alcoholics, fueling their thirst for booze. As the day wore on, and the sun rose higher in the sky, the laughter and chatter grew louder and the adults started acting more and more like uncontrollable children.

Kevin had arrived early and staked out a quiet area, sheltered by trees and far enough away from the crazy crowd that they would have a bit of privacy. He knew he was in a lifelong relationship with Blue Label—but it was a battle. Deep down he also knew that being further away from the crowds, and the booze, would help dampen his "appetite" for the stuff and the crazies that would follow leading to one big, long party. Before he quit drinking, July 4th was an important drinking day. Now it was an important celebration day for different reasons.

Kevin had found a large blanket in the apartment and laid it out. It served as a picnic table and seating for Meg and him; and Sebastian, when he chose to use it. A cooler doubled as a picnic basket and chilled a bottle of "NONALCOHOLIC WINE." *Not too bad for such short notice*, he thought.

"So, Logic Computer Services," Meg said, as she watched Sebastian attack a bone.

Kevin's mind had been in overdrive again, thinking about LCS, the blond thug, the traffic he had intercepted and Julia until he realized Meg was talking to him.

"I'm sorry," he said.

"Logic Computer Services. Can I help you?" Meg asked.

Kevin reached for Sebastian's bone—he growled.

"Not sure," Kevin said. He nodded to Sebastian, "He's pretty protective."

Meg smiled and started to speak—

"So what's your story?" Kevin said. He noticed the blank look on Meg's face, "You know, your AA story?"

She stroked Sebastian.

"Aw, well, you know," she said.

"You really an alcoholic?" Kevin said glancing at the nonalcoholic wine bottle.

Meg reached for Sebastian's bone. He growled again.

"Sorry for being blunt," Kevin said. "But you know the program—it's all about being honest."

"My mother died of cancer when I was seven," Meg said. "My father pretty much raised me and, well, my father," she paused. Tears welled up. She tried to blink them away. "He wanted a boy, and, he got me instead. How could a girl ever live up to those expectations?"

Instinctively, Kevin wiped a tear from Meg's cheek, and then realized what he had done and pulled his hand back. Given her emotional moment, Kevin thought, *maybe she didn't notice what he had just done.*

"His job kept him busy," she said. "By the time I was fourteen, one thing led to another; I was running with a pretty wild crowd." Meg looked at Sebastian, then Kevin and said, "So what about you—your father drive you to drink too?"

Kevin looked away. *We're alcoholics,* he thought. He tried to collect himself. They were talking about her father. It was just a lucky guess

Meg waited for his answer.

"He died a long time ago," Kevin said. "That's all there is to that story."

Meg squirmed as she looked at Sebastian devour the last of his bone.

Kevin watched Meg gently stroke Sebastian's chin, just like Julia.

"So how did you get this fella?" Meg said.

"Long story."

"I'm a good listener."

"He was a present," Kevin said, "on my first AA birthday to be exact." He had never told anyone that. It was a *family* secret he and Julia had. "My," he caught himself, "a friend gave him to me." He stared at the grass, as if counting every blade. "A very special friend."

"Girlfriend?" Meg asked.

She was more to him than anyone could know, he thought, as he sat in silence.

"More," he said. "Someone who stuck with me when no one should've. Accepted me unconditionally, something that I never got from anyone else."

"Acceptance," Meg said as she wiped a tear from her eye, "the root of happiness or sadness. Looks like we have something in common."

Kevin stared at the "NONALCOHOLIC WINE," then turned back to Meg.

Sebastian, the suck, was lying across her lap, enjoying all the attention.

"Among other things," he said.

Meg nodded and continued to stroke Sebastian.

"About LCS," Kevin said, "their financial problems. They've got a bunch of new clients—new clients they don't seem to want anyone to know about."

Meg stopped stroking Sebastian.

"By the way," he said, "you run interference really well."

He noticed Meg had a puzzled look.

"The other night with Paul."

"Oh right," Meg said, nodding her head.

Kevin's eyes darted back and forth searching for unwanted guests, and then he leaned closer to Meg.

"Suppose I told you that I've been destroying LCS data files."

"Just part of your job—right?" Meg responded.

"Routine storage maintenance," Kevin said. He fought the temptation to tell Meg more, and then said, "Normally. But, it's what I discovered. I'm destroying Internet traffic logs for our new clients, in fact the same clients, day in and day out—usually within twenty-four to forty-eight hours of origination."

"What do you think is up?" Meg asked as she started to look around. Kevin's constant glancing around now seemed to have made Meg nervous, as she was doing the very same thing.

"I think it's got something to do with the information moving through LCS." Kevin said.

"How do you figure that?"

"Well, beyond freeing up storage there are only a few of reasons why a company would destroy data traffic logs," Kevin said. "So no one can determine who is routing information through the company, and *no* one can find out where it's going."

He noticed Meg's eyebrows rise.

He had just put those words and information out there—hoping he might get some INTEL from Meg about LCS.

"And let's just be clear, if anyone wanted to see the actual content—emails and text messages, they can forget it," Kevin said.

"No one?" she said. "Not even the government?"

Kevin nodded agreement.

"I'm in," she said.

"Not so fast," Kevin said.

Meg gave Kevin a playful pout.

"I'll think about it," he said. She pouted almost as good a Julia did. While Meg might be able to provide some real good information and could help, he struggled with whether he could trust her or not. The fact she ran interference to save him from Paul's wrath helped swing the pendulum in her favor. "First, I need to figure out what type of information they're moving."

Meg noticed a black car pull up beside Kevin's fifty-seven Chev. She quickly turned back to Kevin.

"Information?" she asked, then jokingly added, "like some sort of covert ops—"

Kevin laughed and said, "Right."

Meg caught a glimpse of the back dark tinted window of the car open. It was Joe Martelli. She shuttered as a chill ran through her spine and she jumped up sending Sebastian flying.

"We should go," she said. "I'm," she gestured at the sun. "I think I got a bit too much sun."

Kevin gazed up at the sun as Meg glanced over her shoulder.

Joe smiled at her as the car window closed and the car slowly rolled away.

CHAPTER 8

KEVIN CATNAPPED ON the couch, while Sebastian snuggled up alongside and the television played in the background. The volume pumped up as a news program started and the host on the television said, "Tonight on the Nations Report, we'll be talking with Shirley, who until recently was in the Federal Witness Protection Program. After her husband was killed, she was released from the program."

"Thanks for giving me a chance to talk about what happens to spouses in the program," Mrs. Wilson said.

Kevin's eyes popped wide open; he knew that voice. He instantly sat up, sending Sebastian to the floor. He stared at Mrs. Wilson's silhouette on the television screen.

"My husband, Donald Wilson, gave testimony that put a horrible man in prison. They killed him and the government could not, did not protect him."

"For those of you who do not remember," the television program host said, "drug lord Anthony Stilleto was sentenced to three hundred and fifty-seven years in prison— Mr. Wilson was the only witness who lived to testify."

Kevin leapt from the couch, dashed to the bedroom, and rifled through a dresser drawer. He pulled out a folder and returned to the living room couch. He studied a newspaper-clipping headline, "WOMAN INNOCENT VICTIM OF DRUG DEAL GONE BAD." His eyes moved down the page and zeroed in on the small type font headline "ATTORNEY GENERAL BELIEVES REVIEW WILL PROVE ANONYMITY NOT COMPROMISED."

He read the first sentence of the article aloud, "Feds in damage control mode as they continue to deny any claims that witness identities are being compromised." Beside the article, there was a photograph of a man named "Spitz."

Kevin bolted for his computer and opened a file. A list of names, addresses and employers splashed across the screen faster than he could read it. After a moment, he zeroed in on one name on the screen, "Donald Wilson, Deceased, aka Jack Spitz." He thought back to that night at the hospital and the hallway conversation he had overheard. *So this is what Martelli wanted to keep quiet, Spitz and Wilson.* They were the same person, a man in the Federal Witness Protection Program who was killed.

* * * * *

Kevin exited a University Medical Center elevator and instinctively glanced up at the surveillance camera—a red light was flashing. As he approached the Nursing Station, the familiar face of the nurse who promised to search for Julia's rings looked up and saw him. The look on her face said it all. Kevin knew she was in shock seeing a man who had risen from the dead. He needed to speak with Mrs. Wilson and the nurse offered hope that he would be able to get an address.

* * * * *

A taxi pulled up in front of the house that hospital records indicated was Mrs. Wilson's residence. He jumped out of the Taxi and surveyed the street and surrounding houses. He knew it would be too much to hope that a black SUV might be parked up the street, watching her every move.

* * * * *

Kevin poured a tea for Mrs. Wilson, as they sat in her living room. Even with all that was happening to her that night at the hospital, she had remembered him. She, however, was not the woman he remembered that night at the hospital. She had transformed into a feisty crusader on a mission.

"They think they can just punt me now that my husband is dead!" she said, as she watched Kevin prepare her tea. "Two lumps of sugar, please. One splash of cream." She politely smiled at Kevin, "They even refused to pay for his funeral."

Kevin handed Mrs. Wilson her tea.

"I knew they'd kill him—damn Justice Department people just kept stalling."

The Justice Department, Kevin thought. The words "Joe Martelli?" flew out of his mouth before he could think anymore about it.

"That's his name!" she replied.

Kevin fought the anger that grew inside him.

"That Martelli fella came by. He seemed like such a sweet young man. He convinced my husband that he should testify and we'd be taken care of for the rest of our lives."

Kevin's stomach turned. Martelli made him sick.

"Newspapers reported that your husband was a confidential informant," Kevin said.

"All my husband wanted to do is tell them what he saw. He wanted it to be confidential, like a confidential informant," Mrs. Wilson said. "Mr. Martelli talked us into the witness protection program. After my husband was killed, Mr. Martelli told me that the papers might get their facts wrong and say he was a confidential informant. It would be best to just let it blow over, rather than attract attention to myself. That's what I did until they kicked me out of the witness protection program. Then I went on television."

Kevin smiled to himself as he sipped his tea. Martelli certainly had not banked on tangling with Mrs. Wilson.

Kevin glanced at his watch. He did not want to be too pushy, but he only had a couple of hours and then he had to start the long drive back to Fort Worth.

"Mrs. Wilson, you mentioned a photograph."

"Two men," she said. "I know they killed him, right at the hospital."

"At the hospital!" Kevin said.

"How else do you explain ingesting a blood thinner," she said, "*in the hospital* while you're bleeding to death?" she shook her head. "It was no accident or coincidence. It was murder."

Mrs. Wilson pointed at a framed photograph hanging on the wall behind Kevin.

"They even stole my husband's wedding ring," she said.

Kevin spun around to look at the photo. He immediately noticed the wedding band.

"Married thirty-eight years next month," she added.

He turned back to Mrs. Wilson and his eyes locked in on the diamond ring and gold band on Mrs. Wilson's finger. The nurse told him she had never located Julia's ring and was quick to recount Mrs. Wilson's incident regarding her husband's wedding band. It also disappeared the night he died and never appeared on the hospital inventory of patient valuables. He was relieved he did not have to ask her about it, but was disgusted at the thought of the sick, twisted person who would do this.

Kevin stared at Mrs. Wilson; the doctor had told him Julia had bled to death. The security camera at the hospital was not working that night. A chill went up his spin.

"The photo—did one of them have blond hair?" Kevin asked.

He saw the surprised look on Mrs. Wilson's face.

"How did you know that?" she said.

Suddenly, as if a fire had been reignited, Mrs. Wilson appeared thirty years younger than she was the night he first met her. She scurried to a desk drawer, pulled out a photo, and waved it in the air, "Got the photo right here."

* * * * *

Kevin studied the photo. It was taken in daylight hours, right in front of the Alexandria Courthouse. One of the men had long blond hair; it was the guy he briefly saw at the gravel pit—the thug that killed Julia. The other man could have been there that night, but he did not recognize him.

"He killed my wife, Mrs. Wilson," Kevin said pointing at the blond haired man in the photograph. "That's the thug that killed my unborn son and I am sure he killed your husband."

* * * * *

The early morning sun was rising and warmed the cemetery grass. It was the time of day Jewels loved most. Kevin blinked away the tears as he stared at one large headstone, "JOSH, JULIA and KEVIN ALBRIGHT, FOREVER A FAMILY, MAY THEY REST IN PEACE." Three fresh roses rested on the headstone.

* * * * *

"Boss, you gotta see this," Hazze said rushing into Big D's office with a computer printout report.

Big D was enjoying a Cuban cigar as he stared out the window. "Hazze, I hope you are bringing some *real* good news."

"It's very interesting, D," Hazze said as he eagerly handed the printout to Big D.

Big D studied the printout and he could not believe what he was reading. It was completely impossible. He looked at Hazze with disbelief.

"Double and tripled checked it, D," Hazze said. "It's the real thing."

CHAPTER 9

S TEELIE WATCHED BIG D pace up one side and down the other of his corner office windows.

Between smoking and munching on the end of his cigar, Big D fumed—cigar smoke swirled around his head.

"So," Steelie said, "the Attorney General's got Albright in Witness Protection."

"He's working at Logic Computer Services," Big D said. He paused to spit out a piece of cigar tobacco. "Our own goddamn Fort Worth company!"

Steelie pulled a chain out from under his shirt and waved it in the air. Julia's rings dangled from it.

Big D looked at the rings; he collected real artifacts and antiques, something with value and a history. Steelie collected "treasurers" from those he had a permanent termination meeting with—rings. He was obsessed with men's rings and women's rings. In Big D's mind, they had little value, except to remind Steelie of one moment of history—the moment he killed them. One other thing he noticed was that more often than not, the treasurers were taken from women. Big D would never keep treasurers like this. If he was caught on some raid, he'd quickly become a prime suspect in hundreds of unsolved cases.

"Another fucking souvenir?" Big D said.

"Nope," Steelie said. "Just unfinished business." He kissed the diamond ring, "Well, sweetie, guess you finally get to see your husband."

"This time, *do* it!" Big D said. "I don't want our associates to start thinking we're changing ISPs like underwear."

Steelie flashed a grin at Big D.

"Since we torched his place, he's probably hiding," Steelie said. "Scared shitless by now." He stuffed the chain back inside his shirt and jumped up to leave.

"Steelie," Big D said, "we're stuck with Logic Computer Services for the moment—keep our associates happy. The last thing we need is for them to get nervous."

* * * * *

Kevin rubbed his eyes. It was another long night staring at his Logic Computer Services computer screen. "JB.traffic23 file retrieved," appeared on the monitor. He hesitated, then slowly stood and scanned the screen partitioned office landscape. Paul was not in his office. *Perfect*, he thought. He was about to read a pile of email he had recently scooped up. He had saved copies of the email that flowed through LCS to a file labeled JB.traffic23. He had the file encrypted in case fellow employees or Paul stumbled upon it. This was highly unlikely, as he had designed a little program to save the file to a hidden folder on his local hard drive. As a further measure, the folder was stored in a hidden drive partition he had created. If someone stumbled on to a discrepancy in the data capacity on the hard drive, any searches would display it as a corrupt partition that was not readable.

Tonight, he was interested in finding out what LCS was handling in the way of traffic for one of their major, growing clients—International Antiques.

Kevin sat back down at his computer and clicked on the JB.traffic23 file.

The system responded with a list of emails.

His eyes scanned the list and zeroed in on one email on the screen, "From International Antiques; Subject: US ORDERS." Kevin opened it.

A list of names splashed across the screen, with addresses and employers.

He quickly realized the list was in alphabetical order. His finger started down the list of "A names." He jumped to the "B's" and zeroed in on one name on the screen, "Josh Burke, alias Kevin Albright, Employer Logic Computer Services."

His instantly rolled back from the computer screen, *holy shit.* His eyes darted around the office and the sweat trickled down his forehead.

* * * * *

Kevin had left his night shift early. He told Paul he suddenly felt ill, probably the result of something he had eaten. He just needed to clear his head and figure out his next steps. It was just a matter of time before those who did not want him to make it to trial to testify would learn that he was still alive, that is, if they did not already know.

One thing was for certain, he would need to contact Wes and make plans to get what little stuff he had out of the apartment.

Kevin hurried into his apartment and threw his jacket on the cigarette burned arm of his couch. He brushed past Sebastian and went straight to the window in his living room. It was open and the curtains flapped in the night breeze. He thought *he might have seen the same vehicle following him a couple times this week; maybe they were already following him home from work—scoping out the place.* Kevin did not see signs of a vehicle. He could not see anything in the extreme blackness. The streetlights were out for some reason.

He rushed to the phone, tripping over Sebastian's chew toys and picked the receiver up and dialed. It rang endlessly as Kevin pleaded with some invisible telephone operator, "Come on, Wes, pickup!" His hair was sweat soaked and it was running down his forehead, cheeks and the back of his neck like a leaky water hose. He wiped the sweat from his forehead. As he waited, his eyes started to burn from the salty sweat running into them.

* * * *

Wes's phone rang. It was the middle of the night, but he was in the office. Joe Martelli was in town and demanded they meet before he returned to Washington, D.C.

Wes glanced at his phone display—"Josh Burke."

"It's Albright," he said motioning to Joe.

"Let it ring," Joe ordered.

* * * * *

Kevin slammed the phone down. The Marshal was not picking up at the office or on his cell phone. So much for memorizing the phone numbers on the Marshal's business card. He slowly surveyed the living room. His eyes landed on the closet door. He fought the temptation to walk to the closet and open the door. He had promised himself that what he had purchased was just for an emergency. He told himself this was not an emergency. He needed to focus on something else.

He turned the television on and slumped down on the couch. In less than a minute, a liquor commercial appeared. This was not a coincidence. It was karma—the alcohol demon was after his soul. He swallowed as he looked at the image of a bottle of "Johnnie Walker Blue Label" as its contents poured into an elegant glass. His eyes glazed over as he fixated on the scotch and ice swishing around in the glass.

Kevin fought the urge. He swallowed hard one last time—then snapped. He leaped up and bolted to the closet. He slid the door open, and pulled out a cardboard box. He ripped it open to reveal an unopened bottle of "Johnnie Walker Blue Label." He had imagined it a thousand times. The excuse was always different, but it ended the same. He would finally have a reason to take a drink. Of course, if he had not bought the bottle, he would have time to fight the temptation. But deep down, he did not want to give himself that chance. His father was right; he was just like him.

* * * * *

Steelie hated airports and flying. And a sixteen-hour drive to Fort Worth had turned his annoyance with Kevin Albright into anger. As he approached the front doors of Kevin's apartment building, he pulled out a small leather case—with tools to unlock doors.

Diggs stepped out of the black SUV and slammed the door.

"Damn it," Steelie said. He glanced back at Diggs, "You want to wake every body in the neighborhood up?"

"Sorry," Diggs said as he stepped up beside Steelie.

"You had better hope Albright's asleep," Steelie said, "a very deep sleep."

Diggs pulled out his gun and clicked a bullet into the chamber as Steelie pulled on the entrance door to Kevin's apartment building. The last person entering or leaving had left the door ajar. It was as if Steelie was being invited in to kill Albright. He stuffed the leather case back in to his jacket pocket.

* * * * *

The curtain blew in the breeze as Kevin peered through the window. He tightly held the unopened bottle of scotch in his right hand. There was a vehicle parked just down the street, an SUV. It was not there earlier. His instincts told him he had to get out of the apartment quickly.

Sebastian must have sensed it too, as he ran up to Kevin and growled.

"Quiet boy," Kevin said as he slowly lowered the scotch bottle to the floor and then muzzled Sebastian with his hand.

He made a beeline to his computer and ejected the hard drive. He never stored data on the resident hard drive with the computer's operating system, and he was not about to let anyone see the contents of his search to find Julia's killers. He stuffed the hard drive into a backpack and slipped in on.

"Let's go boy," he said as they hurried to the door.

* * * * *

Kevin and Sebastian exited the rear door of the apartment building and quickly circled around the block. They slowly approached the SUV—it was black. Kevin peaked through the window and spotted a flashing light. The SUV was equipped with NaviGator. And for a moment, he heard Julia's voice play in his head, "Bet you're glad we have NaviGator now?" He was not glad they had NaviGator—he held it partially responsible for Julia's death. However, NaviGator might have a chance for redemption. He stepped back and studied the antenna, then snapped it off. He hoped this little maneuver would come in handy later.

Sebastian barked.

Kevin turned to Sebastian, his tail was wagging; he was ready to fetch the newly found "stick." Kevin dove for cover.

* * * * *

Steelie peered through the window from Kevin's apartment and spotted Sebastian. "Just the neighbor's dog," he whispered to Diggs.

* * * * *

Kevin rushed to the rear of SUV. He wanted to check out the license plate. Part of him hoped it would be a match. The other part of him hoped it was not as a match meant they were close—very close to getting him.

Mud covered the last three characters of the license plate. Kevin kicked the mud off to reveal the full plate number, "6T0 9W5." *Finally gotch*a, he thought. He grabbed Sebastian by the collar and hustled him down the street. They hid behind an evergreen hedge and waited for the driver to return to the SUV.

Kevin watched as Diggs hurried out of the apartment complex and jumped into the SUV. The man was big, big enough to have been one of the men who were at the gravel pit when Julia was shot. However, Kevin could not be sure. He was sure of one thing: there was a blond-haired thug, and he would know him anywhere. If he was here tonight, he had not come out the front entrance.

After a few minutes, the SUV drove down the block. A silhouette of someone walking out of the back alley appeared. Within seconds, the tall figure jumped into the back of the SUV before Kevin could make them out.

* * * * *

As the morning sun broke through the apartment living room window, Kevin stepped over broken furniture to examine his computer. All that remained was a busted computer monitor oozing the contents of a smashed Johnnie Walker Blue Scotch bottle that lay beside it.

* * * * *

Wes leaned back in his squeaky chair. He was on the telephone with the FBI.

"Listen Agent Wells," Wes said, "Albright's been calling all morning, I'm going to have to tell him something."

"Stall him," Wells said. "Tell him we're pursuing new leads, but we've got nothing to share with him."

"He's not going to like the answer," Wes said as he started to hang up.

"And Marshal," Wells said, "tell Albright he is not to contact anyone at the FBI under any circumstances."

"Why?" Wes asked.

Click. Agent Wells hung up.

Wes's line went dead. He immediately dialed a number, "Come on, Josh—pick up." But there was no answer.

* * * * *

Kevin entered the smoke-filled AA meeting room. Like any other meeting night, the room was packed as he searched the crowd for Meg. She was not there.

* * * * *

The next morning, Kevin was crammed into a phone booth outside a motel. The top half of the phone booth still had glass, while plywood replaced the glass on the bottom half of the phone booth. He cradled the phone receiver under his chin as he searched for a coin.

The motel was a dive, no phones in the rooms, not even a phone in the lobby, if you could call it a lobby. Rooms rented out by the hour and half day. It gave the term seedy motel a completely new meaning. Even on his worst binge, he had not landed in a dive like this. He found a coin, and dialed Wes's number.

"Marshal Kindrake's Office," the receptionist said.

"Is he in?" Kevin said.

"I'm sorry he's not available at the moment."

Kevin heard a vehicle pull into the motel parking lot; he ducked down behind the plywood-covered bottom to hide. He peered out through the glass. It was just a pimp dropping off a hooker. He watched as she straightened her butt-covering skirt and went into the motel lobby.

"Hello—" the receptionist said in a louder voice.

Kevin jumped; he had momentarily forgotten he was on the phone, worried that the vehicle could have been the black SUV or a vehicle with a blond haired passenger.

"Yes, I'm still here," he said.

"If you give me your name and a number, I'll get the message to Marshal Kindrake," the receptionist said.

"Just tell him Josh, no, Kevin Albright called."

"Oh, Mr. Burke," the receptionist said. "He needs to talk to you when he's—"

Kevin slammed the receiver down.

"When he's free," Kevin said finishing the sentence himself.

After a moment, he picked the receiver up again, loaded a coin, and dialed. Frustrated after half a dozen rings, he canceled the call, reloaded a coin and dialed. It was answered on the second ring.

"Meg?" Kevin said.

"No," the LCS receptionist said. "Meg's not available at the moment. Josh, is that you?"

Kevin hung up. He started to dial again, and then realized he needed to drop another coin in to the hungry pay phone. He loaded a coin and dialed. One ring and was answered.

"Agent Wells," Kevin said instantly.

"He's in a meeting at the moment," the FBI receptionist said.

Kevin slammed the receiver down so hard it fell off the hook and swung like a hanging gallows.

He took a deep breath and dug a piece of paper out of his pocket. He glanced at Sebastian. He was sure Sebastian sensed his panic. But he followed Kevin's command, sat and dutifully watched his master.

"Well, boy," Kevin said.

Sebastian's tail responded and he immediately stood, waiting for instructions.

"Guess we gotta do this," Kevin said reaching for the receiver.

CHAPTER 10

AGENT JENSEN FLIPPED through a file at his desk. Colombia was still in a coma, and without other witnesses to the gravel pit shoot out, he had been cleared to ease back into full duty. Right now, his foot was still sore. He spent his days on light administrative duties—no field work, at least not that his superiors knew of. He paused to look at his partner.

Agent Murray pulled a hair out of his nose and winced.

Jensen shook his head and laughed to himself just as the phone rang. He looked at the phone. It rang again. He gave Murray a nod to pick it up.

Murray's eyes watered as he picked up the phone, "Special Agent Murray."

"Is Agent Jensen in?" Kevin said.

"Who is this?" Agent Murray said.

"Tell him it's," Kevin said. There was a pause, then, "Kevin. Kevin Albright."

Murray jerked to attention and covered the mouthpiece of the receiver with one hand.

"Darrel!" Murray said in a low voice.

Agent Darrel Jensen ignored Murray.

"Darrel," Murray said again as he frantically waved his hand to get Jensen's attention.

Annoyed, Jensen finally looked up at Murray. Once they started working for Steelie and Big D, Murray had a tough time holding it together, and since Julia Albright's death on their watch, everything seemed to rattle Murray—even a simple phone call.

"It's Albright!" Murray said.

Jensen sat straight up. Did he just hear Murray right?

"Albright," Jensen said. It was not a question. Albright was dead and buried. It was an attempt to clarify that Murray had not misspoke.

Agent Murray nodded yes.

Jensen grabbed the phone and covered the mouthpiece. He took a deep breath and motioned to Murray to continue talking to Kevin.

"Mr. Albright," Murray said, "Special Agent Jensen and I thought you were dead."

"Seems you might be the only ones," Kevin said.

Jensen motioned to Murray; he would take the call.

"Mr. Albright, Special Agent Jensen here. I was just taking care of some paperwork. Where are you?"

"Getting the guy who killed my wife," Kevin said.

Jensen motioned to Murray to trace the call.

Murray switched lines. "This is Special Agent Murray," he said in a low voice. "I need a trace on line two."

"Mr. Albright, I want to help you," Jensen said.

Murray listened back in on his partner's conversation with Kevin.

"I know you tried to save Julia's life," Kevin said. "And for that, I'm grateful. I also know that the same people may have killed your daughter. You probably want them as much as I do, but now it's my turn."

There was a long moment of silence.

Jensen exchanged a look of astonishment with Murray. How could Kevin know that? How could he have pieced any of this together?

"That's not why I'm calling," Kevin continued. "You guys have a major leak in your organization."

"A leak?" Jensen said.

"Yep," Kevin replied. "Someone in your organization is leaking Witness Protection files."

"What?" Jensen said, leaping out of his chair. Like he had just been shot again, a sharp pain flashed through his body as he realized what he had just done. He fell back into his chair. The pain caused his eyes to water. He wiped away the tears and looked at Murray.

"Believe it," Kevin continued, "and the files are being distributed over the Internet."

Jensen stared out into space as he digested what he had just heard. All the hard work, all the effort to get close to Big D was about to go down the toilet.

"Agent Jensen, are you still there?" Kevin said.

"Where are you?" Jensen said as he glanced at Murray— the guy was freaking out. "We'll come and get you." Jensen waited for Kevin to answer. There was only silence and then he said, "Mr. Albright?"

"Just deal with your problem!" Kevin said.

Jensen heard the click of the phone. Kevin had hung up. Jensen stared at his phone. All he heard was a dial tone.

* * * * *

Special Agent Larson watched on as his partner paced their D.C. FBI Field Office and ranted. He had never seen Agent Wells this upset.

"Albright held out on us. He should have told us about the man he talked to," Wells said. "We've lost another potential witness."

Wells was right. A check of phone calls to the Wayne Helmes residence that night brought up a call from a cell phone that fit the timeframe. It turned out to be a burner cell. Further investigation indicated the cell had been purchased a week before the call was made and the call to the Helmes residence was the only call made from that cell.

"And what about that barricade—again he held out on us. What the fuck else did he forget to tell us?" Wells said.

Larson started to speak, but Wells was not finished.

"And now—how do you lose someone in witness protection?" Wells said. "All Kindrake had to do was baby-sit Albright. No wonder Wit Pro is in such a fucking mess."

Larson knew his partner was right again. The U.S. Marshal's Service was charged with protecting federal witnesses, and that meant keeping tabs on them. In Kevin Albright's case, Marshal Wes Kindrake was responsible. They needed Albright, alive, and ready to testify at the Rodriguez Garcia trial. Albright had some explaining to do and if Wells was even half-right, they would discover that Jensen and Murray played a bigger role at the gravel pit shoot-out then they were admitting. Unfortunately, without more evidence, some of which Albright might be holding back, Jensen and Murray would continue to appear to be heroes to those who wanted drugs off the street.

"Looks like Jensen and Murray are walking," Larson said.

Larson watched Wells as he stopped in his tracks. He knew he had hit a nerve.

"Not yet Larson," Wells said. "Not yet."

* * * * *

Special Agent Murray rushed out of the FBI D.C. Field Office Building.

A moment later, Agent Jensen hobbled out of the building and yelled, "Murray."

Murray stopped and waited for his handicapped partner to catch up.

Jensen gritted his teeth and winced with each step he took until he was face-to-face with Murray. Then Murray spun and took a step.

Jensen grabbed Murray by his suit jacket, "It's the middle of the day; you want someone to see you like this?"

Murray snapped his suit jacket coattail out of Jensen's hand.

"Now, let's walk to the car," Jensen said. He paused and then enunciated the next word. "Slowly."

* * * * *

Agent Jensen was taking painkillers, but he believed he was certainly in better shape than Murray was to be driving. Truthfully, at the moment, he did not trust Murray to do anything. He drove their car as fast as he could without attracting attention, to put some distance between them and the D.C. Field Office. He hit the brakes and cranked the wheel hard, pulling into a back alley. Seconds later, he threw the car into park. He watched Murray wipe the sweat from his forehead.

"We're sunk," Murray said.

Jensen was annoyed. "Jesus, Eric!" he said. If he thought he could get away with it, he would have killed Murray right there and then. But he needed to get his daughter's killers and unfortunately, that meant not attracting any more attention, for now. Besides, Murray had been the perfect partner for him. No other agent would be a party to breaking the law and put their career on the line. He certainly did not want to make any more waves with Steelie, as he needed to get to Big D.

"Albright's alive," Murray said. "Who knows what he's discovered?"

"Maybe it wasn't Albright," Jensen said.

"Right, maybe Agent Wells is yanking our chain." Murray said, as he pulled out his cell phone. He started dialing.

"Now what the hell are you doing?" Jensen said.

"Letting Steelie know," Murray said.

Jensen grabbed the cell from Murray and tossed it out the window to the pavement.

"I put my job on the line—nearly got killed," Jensen said. "Now I'm close to getting Big D and you want to jeopardize it all!" He started the car, jammed the gearshift into reverse and slowly backed up until he could see Murray's cell phone on the pavement. Then he threw the gearshift into drive and punched the accelerator. He aimed the car's front tire at Murray's cell and made sure he drove over the cell, smashing it. He locked up the brakes and backed up over the cell. "Get out," Jensen said to Murray.

Murray stared at Jensen.

"Get out—now." Jensen said.

"But Darrel," Murray said.

"Get out and grab the damn phone," Jensen said. "We don't want to leave any evidence behind."

* * * * *

Kevin worked the kinks out of his neck. It was approaching midnight and he had been restless and unable to sleep in the poor excuse for a motel bed. He had spent the last couple of hours driving around, afraid to stop long in any one place. He grabbed the odd catnap in the front seat of his fifty-seven Chev. It was not as comfortable as he remembered back when he and Julia would crash after a night of partying. However, it was still more comfortable than the motel mattress that bowed so much in the middle, his butt nearly touched the floor.

Kevin believed Steelie was still in the Fort Worth area trying to hunt him down. At least, that is what he prayed for earlier as he prepared to confront Steelie. *This time he would be calling the shots—the surprise attack would be his,* he thought as he took a deep breath, grabbed his cell and dialed. As he waited for his call to be answered, he looked at the basic cell he now owned—*if it were a smartphone, they would be tracking him already*

"One moment," the operator said and instantly put him on hold. *Just his luck, a busy night at NaviGator,* Kevin thought. It seemed that nothing was going to be easy about tonight.

As he waited for the operator, he studied a computer report, the most recent fruit of his hacking efforts. It included the details of Steelie's vehicle, "Model: SUV Color: Black, Registered To: Carlos Steelie License Plate 6T0 9W5, PIN: The last four digits of phone no. on file." Kevin smiled to himself. For such a sophisticated operation, the security password was rudimentary.

"Good evening, NaviGator. How may I help you?" the operator said.

"Hello, my name is Carlos Steelie," Kevin said. "I know it's late, but I need to get to a very important meeting and I've encountered technical problems downloading directions to my GPS."

"Mr. Steelie," the operator said, "we need to confirm your PIN number."

Kevin ran his finger down the page and located the phone number on the report.

"The last four digits of my phone number are 9164."

Moments later, Kevin and the NaviGator operator were in mid-discussion as he tried to explain the nature of the technical problem he was experiencing with his NaviGator service.

"Had it parked outside a bar," Kevin said. "Some drunk must have snapped the antenna off."

Kevin waited for the operator to respond. He had done his best to convince her of the dilemma he was in. He hoped it was enough; otherwise, his plan was dead in the water.

"Well, we have you at the corner of Miramar and Rice," the operator said.

"That's correct," Kevin said as he did a celebratory fist pump.

"To get to Logic Computer Services, you need to stay on Miramar, and turn left at the Express Way, and then take the third exit," the operator said.

"Thanks very much," Kevin replied.

"Mr. Steelie, your account states that we are to bill you for additional services as used," the operator said.

Kevin laughed on the inside at the irony of this, as he thought about the many ways he wanted to make Steelie pay for what he had done to his family. Putting the charges on Steelie's tab would be one more way.

"Absolutely," Kevin said. "Getting to the meeting on time is worth it."

Kevin tossed his cell on the floor. While smartphones were easy targets in cyberspace, anyone out to kill him would soon have a trace on his basic cell too. It was just a matter of time before they hacked the cell and turned it into a listening device. It would be like having a police wire taped to his body to record a conversation with the criminals, only this time, the criminals would have *the invisible wire.* The phone would become a microphone. The criminals could be a thousand miles away and turn it on and it would broadcast every sound made in the cell phone's proximity back to the criminals. They could listen to everything the cell holder was doing, even though the cell holder was not even talking to anyone on the phone.

In the case of smartphones, Kevin knew all of this was even easier because a smartphone was a powerful miniature computer that could be wirelessly hacked, programmed and operated from anywhere in the world. That was another reason why Kevin refused to use a smartphone. He maintained that, in the wrong hands, they were more dangerous than a gun. A gun fires one bullet at a time—a smartphone could launch a global network of invisible bullets—punch one button, fire a million bullets. In the wrong hands, hi-jacked smartphones make the efforts of the firearms lobby look like a church group lobbying for the right to buy and use squirt guns on a hot day at a Sunday picnic.

CHAPTER 11

KEVIN ARRIVED AT the downtown intersection of Miramar and Rice and pulled to the curb. He surveyed the street. The black SUV was still there, but the headlights were on and it was about to pull away from the curb into traffic.

He reached into the glove box and pulled out a Smith and Wesson .500 Magnum revolver. The Model 29 had an 8 3/8 inch barrel. As he snapped the cylinder open and double-checked it to ensure it was loaded, he felt like Dirty Harry—even though he did not choose the make or model of gun.

While he hated to admit it, the AA network occasionally had some fringe benefits. Those with a criminal past who were at their weakest point were desperate to get honest and make amends. He had recently met one such member at an AA meeting in Fort Worth and he agreed to take the Smith and Wesson revolver off his hands. He flipped the cylinder closed. It was loaded with six bullets, and tonight he only needed one to take care of business.

* * * * *

Kevin's fifty-seven Chev maneuvered through traffic and pulled up alongside the black SUV. He prayed that Steelie was behind the wheel, but he could not see anything or anyone through the SUV's dark tinted windows. It was like the veil and shield of the Internet. No one could see whom they were dealing with or what they were doing. For all he knew, Steelie was pointing a gun at him, but it was a chance he had to take.

Diggs was behind the wheel of the black SUV and casually glanced over at the fifty-seven Chev and turned back to watch the car in front of him. In an instant, his head spun to the left and he looked again at the Chevy's driver. There was Kevin Albright, the man Steelie was hunting down. Diggs pulled a gun out of his shoulder holster.

"Mr. Albright, this time you die," he uttered.

The tinted driver's window smoothly and quickly opened to reveal Diggs. He flashed a Heckler Custom Compact handgun at Kevin.

"Where's Steelie?" Kevin growled to himself. He was disappointed. Then he realized this was the man he saw exit his apartment complex the night his apartment was trashed. He remembered another man jumping in the backseat of the SUV. He needed that man to be Steelie and more than ever tonight, he needed him to be riding in the SUV. He would kill them both.

Diggs flashed his Heckler again in Kevin's face and grinned at him.

That was it; Kevin flashed his larger .500 Magnum back at Diggs and yelled, "You're a dead man!" He tucked the magnum at his side and cranked the steering wheel hard right into the SUV.

Diggs flashed a smile and said, "Bring it on Albright!" as he cranked the wheel hard left into Kevin's fifty-seven Chev.

Kevin countered and cranked his steering wheel harder to the right.

Pedestrians ran for cover as the vehicles crashed and rubbed against each other in a duel down the street.

Kevin stared down Diggs for more than five seconds. He forced himself to glance ahead. A mother and young boy were in the middle of the street. He frantically cranked the steering wheel to the left to avoid them.

The fifty-seven Chev bounced onto the sidewalk.

He fought with the steering wheel to avoid crashing into a concrete building and ran the car along the entire length of a building's brick exterior. Sparks flew in every direction. It looked like an out-of-control metal grinder was attacking the Chev as it approached an intersection.

Diggs locked up the brakes of the SUV sending it into 180-degree spin.

An old Cadillac Seville crawled into the intersection in front of Kevin. It was too close and he knew he could not avoid it. The Caddy launched the Chev into orbit, sending it crashing into another vehicle. It felt like the tilt-a-wheel he and Julia rode at the state fair; except this time, there were no rails to control the trajectory of the ride.

* * * * *

Kevin was dazed, but conscious. An adrenaline fueled survival instinct kicked in and his heart pounded against his chest to escape, as he struggled to get out of the fifty-seven Chev. It was built with transportation, not safety, in mind, but he had survived. The old cars had more steel bracing and metal in them then the new aluminum, plastic and fiberglass models. He could not open the door. Then he realized the Chev was on its side and he had been trying to force the driver's door open.

He had to go out the passenger window. He crawled up to the passenger window. *Where was his gun?* He needed his gun or he would die for sure in the next moment. He turned and looked back; it was lying against the driver's door. He dropped back inside the Chev and grabbed the gun.

He poked his head out of the passenger door and saw the black SUV accelerating toward him. He squeezed through the passenger window of his mangled Chev, dropped to the pavement and scrambled to get back on his feet. He glanced up at the SUV. It was barreling down on him like a hearse racing to pick a body before it cooled.

Kevin bolted down the street.

The SUV gained on Kevin as Diggs hung his gun out the window. It was like a gunfight at high noon, only on steroids.

Kevin looked over his shoulder and saw the SUV out of the corner of his eye. He whipped around and emptied the .500 Magnum into the driver's side of the SUV. It crashed into a "Liquor Mart" and exploded.

Moments later, Kevin tried to get closer to the SUV. He needed to know if Steelie was in the SUV. The fire kept growing and before he could see who was in the back seat, he heard emergency vehicles closing in.

He sprinted down the block and turned to take one last look for signs of life. Flames totally engulfed the SUV. The gas tank exploded, signaling total destruction. Kevin turned

toward the sky, looking beyond the moon and the stars—
into the heavens.

"That's one, Jewels," he said.

* * * * *

Kevin rushed into his dark motel room and slammed the
door. He fumbled for the light switch. He felt like he
had just gotten out of a swimming pool. His shirt was
drenched from the sweat. He ran his fingers through his hair
and wrung them toward the floor like a mop.

Sebastian jumped down from the bed, and shook himself to wake up. He ran up to Kevin and waited for an
acknowledgement.

Kevin fought for air, trying to catch his breath. He had
walked and run for more than an hour to get here—a cheap
motel room far away from downtown. Kevin dropped onto
the edge of the bed and looked around the room. How did
he ever end up here—a broken down motel room, no
phone, a crappy bed, on the run, no family and now he'd
killed a man—while he was sober to boot?

Sebastian walked up to his master and waited for the
command to sit.

Instead Kevin stood.

After a moment he slowly walked to the window and
cracked the curtain open. It was pitch black. Even the street-
light near the motel was out. Up until now, he had only
fought in the back alleys; and that was only when he was in
a drunken stupor fighting to protect his next drink. While
he had been close to killing a man when he was drinking,

he had never killed a man. If he was being totally honest, he never killed a man—at least that he could remember. Until Julia was killed, he had never done anything "stupid" when he was sober. *Maybe now was a good time to drink.* He was not sad—he was glad he had killed a man. Maybe he should celebrate. He shook his head. These were the alcohol demons talking again. They were determined to win over his mind and then send his soul to hell.

As the minutes went by, Kevin's anxiety grew, as the alcohol demon seemed to be winning. He was disappointed at how weak he was becoming, second by second. He looked around the room at the nightstand where a phone once sat. Beside it was a hole in the wall where a telephone outlet once existed. Maybe another drunk had been in this room before, and out of frustration with his demons, he had thrown the phone across the room with such force it pulled the outlet right out of the wall. This was crazy thinking and Kevin knew it. He needed to do something quickly, or he would be dead.

He pulled out his cell phone and dialed a number, and listened to it ring. *Please be there,* he thought to himself. He needed to talk to someone about what he had just done. Maybe they would convince him not to take that first drink. It rang again, and then someone answered.

"Meg?' he said.

"Yes," Meg said.

There was a long silence. He could hear her breathing on the other end of the line.

"Josh, are you OK?" she said.

Kevin did not respond.

"Josh—" she said again.

"Just dueled it out with a thug." Kevin said. "He tried to kill me—"

"I'm coming over," she said.

"I'm not at the apartment," Kevin said as he looked around the room. "I'm at a motel."

* * * * *

There was a knock at Kevin's motel room door. Wired, Kevin launched himself up from a wooden chair. He peered through the peephole. It was Meg. He opened the door and started pacing.

Meg stepped in, glanced behind her, and then closed the door.

"Somebody just tried to kill you?" she said.

"They've got my name," Kevin said, "came to my place, tried to kill me—"

"Who?" Meg asked.

"Thugs!" Kevin said. "My name's on a list circulating on the Internet."

"What list?" Meg asked.

Kevin thought about what he had done and what he was about to tell Meg. He had to take a leap of faith and he hoped he could trust Meg—the next few minutes and hours of his not drinking depended on it.

"I just killed one of them!" Kevin said.

Meg slowly walked toward Kevin.

He looked at the floor; not wanting to make eye contact, then started rotating his head in a circular motion to relieve the tension in his neck. He slowly scanned the room and his eyes landed on the broken telephone outlet—broken just like his life was. The likelihood that the room was bugged was slim, and he certainly did not want to be out in public now—there, he was even a bigger target. There might be one redeeming feature about the motel, at least that is what he counted on—no one would think to look for him in such a dive. It was so far off the beaten path.

Kevin stared at Meg for a long moment. He had to tell someone, and Meg did answer his phone call.

"What I'm about to tell you has to stay in this room," he said.

Meg nodded.

"We'd better start at the beginning," Kevin said, "the very beginning. My name isn't Josh Burke. It's really Kevin Albright."

Kevin proceeded to tell Meg about Julia, her killers and his placement in the Federal Witness Protection Program. He stayed guarded about sharing everything with Meg, but she would certainly have a better sense of what he had been going through.

* * * * *

When he finished, Kevin looked at Meg as she sat beside him on the bed. He could tell from the look on her face she was concerned, but he thought it had more too do with the fact she feared he would drink.

She held up a crumpled printout.

"These people are in the Witness Protection Program? You're in the program?"

"Yup," Kevin replied.

"This list is circulating on the Internet?"

Kevin nodded yes.

"Through LCS," he added. "That's how I found it."

"You've got to go to the authorities," Meg said.

"Right now, I just need to not feel—to stop feeling life," Kevin said. *There, I finally said it.* It was what she was probably thinking—have a drink, stop feeling. He certainly was.

Meg put her arm around Kevin.

He tried not to look at Meg, but her eyes drew him closer.

She leaned in so close her breath warmed his ear.

The damn insanity of the drink, he thought, as he moved closer.

"It won't help get these guys," she whispered.

CHAPTER 12

MEG STARED OUT the motel window—the thumping of a headboard against the room next door started again. She glanced at her watch, a new client in less than an hour; it must be a record—a display of a pitiful attempt to please "men" with her body over her mind.

Minutes later, a prostitute ran from a motel room to a waiting taxi. The crow's-feet that framed her blue eyes were more visible, a physical sign of the stress caused by the double life she had led, trying to measure up to the expectations of a man's world.

Now for a few minutes, the morning sun felt nice on her face. She rubbed her stiff back. It could use the warmth. *What had she gotten herself into? Was her life all about still trying to please her father?*

She had not slept all night—partly because of her job. She felt like she was carrying the weight of the world on her shoulders. Then she looked at the empty dilapidated bed— partly because of the bed. The bed frame was rickety and lacked any support system to hold up the poor excuse for a mattress. How did ladies of the night work with in these conditions? she wondered. When she tried lying down in the middle of the bed, her buttocks nearly touched the floor. Worse yet, it gave her a sense that if she fell asleep, the mattress would fold around her and smother her to death.

She glanced up at the ceiling tiles. In the sunlight, their rust stained finish looked like a poor watercolor painting. The only thought that came to mind was *what a hellhole*. Then she looked at Kevin, he had finally fallen asleep an hour ago on a wooden chair. Meg could not suppress her thoughts about what Kevin had been dragged into and she felt sick about the whole situation. This was not what she had signed up for and she knew she had to do something to save what little bit of a life Kevin had left before it was too late.

Kevin stirred, and glanced around the room.

Meg watched him and for a brief moment. It looked like he was not sure where he was.

"Meg," he said after he saw her standing in the window light.

Meg put her finger up to her lips to silence Kevin. She walked to the door and turned to face him.

"I've got something I need to do," she said, "something I should have done a long time ago." She noticed Kevin was about to speak and put her finger to her lips again. "I'll call you later," she said. She had to go as the look in Kevin's eyes only left her feeling sicker. She turned away as she opened the door.

"Thanks," Kevin said.

Damn it, Meg thought. She would not get away without Kevin seeing her face one more time. She turned and nodded. It was the least she could do for Kevin. Inside, guilt was winning the war for control of her emotions. She hoped that Kevin did not notice.

"For being here," he continued as he looked into her eyes. "I don't know what I would have done if you hadn't answered the phone."

"Went to a meeting," Meg said. "Right?"

* * * * *

Kevin stared at a man lying in a pool of blood in a back alley. Beside him laid a Glock 37. Finally, he had to accept it. Now he had seriously wounded or killed two men, one when he was drunk to protect his *lady*—a bottle of scotch, and one when he was sober, in an effort to get Julia's killers.

The first time he felt little emotion when it happened, he was drunk. The second time he felt no remorse or guilt, only a sense of satisfaction that he had confronted one of Julia's killers and he did it sober.

Then another image flashed before his eyes. It was of a man lying in a pool of blood in a bedroom. It was his father; he was holding a Glock 37 in his right hand.

* * * * *

"Kevin," Meg said, "you going to be OK?" Kevin snapped back into the moment.

"My father," he said. He noticed Meg's puzzled look. "You asked about my father. He committed suicide and I chose to drink. Crazy thinking—I thought he betrayed my mother and me. A man doesn't abandon his family."

"You know crazy thinking," Meg said. "Did you ever think he got frustrated at not being able to get sober? Maybe he thought his only choices were to drink and hurt you more or just end it so you could move on as a family."

* * * * *

Special Investigators Palmer and Burgess stood at a whiteboard in Martelli's office. They were briefing Joe Martelli on what they had discovered about the growing death rates in the Federal Witness Protection Program.

Joe studied the whiteboard headed up "OPPROTECT WHAT WE KNOW TO DATE." His eyes slowly dropped to a subheading "WITNESS PROTECTION PROGRAM DEATHS" and then to a series of newspaper clippings taped to the whiteboard. Two headings jumped out at him, "WITNESSES MURDERED" and "STILLETO TRIAL." He slammed his pen down on a notepad on the table and then glared at Palmer and Burgess.

"This is the best you can do?" he said. "There's no way we're taking this pathetic update to the Attorney General."

"We've got to get him out of Logic Computer Services," Meg yelled as she barged in.

"I'm in the middle of a meeting right now," Joe said.

"They're going to kill him," Meg replied.

Joe slowly pushed his chair back from the table and stood. He approached Meg, grabbed her arm and started to escort her to the door.

"We'll talk about this later," Joe said.

"We've got a guy in protection," Meg said. "They tried to kill him last night, and you want to talk later."

Meg tried to get Joe's *paws* off her, but he was not letting go. He had to get her out of the office quickly; the last thing he wanted was to have Palmer and Meg in the same room talking.

"Witness Protection?" Palmer said.

Damn it, Joe thought. It was too late.

"Yes!" Meg said.

"I think we need to hear this," Palmer said as he looked at Burgess, "Don't you?"

Burgess nodded.

Joe grudgingly released Meg's arm.

* * * * *

Joe was totally pissed off, as he stared out the window. He was not impressed that Meg had spilled her guts to Palmer and Burgess, potentially ruining his plans. The last thing he needed was someone, a woman no less, derailing his career.

Joe turned to Palmer. He did not like the way Palmer rocked back and forth in *his* chair, at *his* desk, probably reflecting on a payback to Joe for choking off their lines of direct communication with the Attorney General. Joe had screened, curtailed and stalled their briefings, to buy time to get his own INTEL on problems with the Justice Department's computer security.

Palmer abruptly stopped rocking and looked at Joe.

"Information brokering," he said, and then he turned to Burgess. "This is our goddamn smoking gun!"

Joe spun around and glared at Meg. She was still standing at the door. There was no way in hell he would let her get one step further into *his* office; or feel the least bit comfortable.

"You're still on our team, right?" Joe said to Meg as he stammered with rage.

"I took the assignment, didn't I? The job at Logic—joined his local AA group, tried to get close to Albright. You saw it for yourself at the park," Meg said.

Palmer looked at Joe, shook his head, and turned back to Meg,

"The guy's lost his wife," Meg said. "His identity and now—"

"Maybe you need to step back, get away, take a—" Burgess said to Meg.

"I just don't think it's worth him getting seriously hurt," Meg said.

"You mean killed!" Palmer said.

Joe walked back to the table and surveyed the information scattered across it, and picked up a clipping "WITNESS PROTECTION PROGRAM DEATHS." He held it up and pointed at it.

"The Protection Program is in jeopardy—" Joe said.

"Right, not to mention the Attorney General's reputation," Meg said. Then she marched to the table and picked up a clipping "AG UNDER FIRE."

Joe turned his back on Meg, looked at Palmer and Burgess, and said, "We can't lose sight of the big picture here."

"Oh, I think I get the picture all right," Meg said. "Kevin's life is expendable to save reputations, and personal agendas. Right, Martelli?"

"He didn't say that," Palmer said as he slowly got to his feet. "Let's not lose perspective here on what we're trying to do. You, us, we're here to uphold the law. Burke," he caught himself, "Kevin Albright, wants to catch the people who killed his wife."

"He thinks he's hiding out until the Garcia trial," Meg said.

Joe scowled at Meg and said, "He's the best in his field—"

"And we're using him!" Meg said, as she scowled back at Joe. "Whatever happened to protecting innocent lives?"

"Why, Special Investigator Taylor, that's exactly what we're doing," Joe said.

Meg looked at Palmer and Burgess, and then motioned toward Joe. "Let me guess. You agree with him."

She waited for a response.

Palmer and Burgess opted for silence.

"Right," Meg said.

"We've got a job to do, Investigator Taylor," Burgess said.

"And that's what we're going to do," Palmer added.

Meg turned to Joe.

"I think you'd better get back to work," Joe said. "You know, the job you're paid by the government to do?"

Meg stormed out of the office.

"Close the door on your way out," Joe yelled.

Meg came back, grabbed the doorknob and slammed the door so hard the pictures rattled on the wall.

CHAPTER 13

KEVIN SAT AT his LCS computer monitor. He constantly looked over his shoulder. While the LCS facility was supposed to be a secured facility, he could not trust anyone except Meg and she did not come in tonight. From what he overheard in a telephone conversation Paul had, she was called away on an urgent family matter.

Kevin knew he had little choice but to come to work at LCS tonight. Not showing up would probably be enough to tip off Steelie that he was on to them. Diggs was dead. He was sure that Steelie did not know he had located the SUV and followed it—Diggs didn't have time to alert Steelie about Kevin. He had his hands full trying to kill him.

The newspaper reports indicated that Diggs' death was still under investigation, but it appeared to be associated with drugs. They mentioned that Diggs had been involved in the drug trade in Central America.

Kevin wondered if the FBI or DEA, or the Attorney General for that matter, really believed this, or perhaps "planted it" to deflect attention away from the Attorney General. Any way you sliced and diced it, they were sadly misinformed. Kevin believed that LCS was still his best opportunity to find another lead on Steelie's activities and whereabouts.

Kevin grew even more anxious as he activated "OPEN" on an electronic file. Every time he did this, he was never sure what information he was going to uncover—maybe even plans about the hit on him would appear. He watched as information splashed across the computer screen, "INTERNET TRAFFIC LOG - NIGHT OPS." Two emails jumped out at him—Hazze@InternationalAntiques; iman@InternationalAntiques."

There was that reference again to International Antiques. He had tried to access the International Antiques account details at LCS. They were an LCS client. That was the way their International Antiques domain name was registered. But it appeared that LCS did not maintain any information about this company in their computer systems or databases.

This meant the information he wanted had to be somewhere in Paul's office, most likely in his offline paper files. Kevin had already tried sneaking into Paul's office to check the file cabinets. Paul had called in sick. Kevin believed he had the full nightshift to find an opportunity to slip into his office. He had decided to sit back and wait for the perfect moment. In other words, he delayed as long as he thought he could, only to regret it. He should have gone early at the first chance he had.

Just as he was heading for Paul's office, Paul appeared and he narrowly escaped being caught red-handed by Paul. He was getting better at lying, but there was no way he could have talked his way out of that predicament. He was not sure what prompted Paul to come in that night, perhaps he was getting suspicious, and it was just a matter of time before Paul would just explode and fire him on the spot. Or maybe his new investor was on his case again—demanding more illegal services that only he could deliver.

As Kevin studied the computer screen, he could feel the hairs rise on the back of his neck as he read the information. His intuition told him something was not right—danger was lurking in cyberspace. A look of concern grew on his face. The cursor flashed at him like a warning light at a line that read, "iman@InternationalAntiques." He hit ENTER on his keyboard, immediately the system responded with a computer prompt, "RUN PROCEDURE – DELETE." Kevin knew if he accepted the command, the traffic log and emails would be instantly erased from LCS's records. His added personal procedure was to copy the log and emails first. He erased the "DELETE" command and typed, "COPY TO USB FLASH DRIVE."

His fingers froze as he looked around the office. No one was in sight. He hit ENTER on the keyboard, and glanced down at the USB flash drive. The USB drive lights flashed as files were copied to it. He would study the information details later once he got back to his motel room.

* * * * *

Meg stared out her apartment window at the lit up Fort Worth night skyline. She could not stop thinking about Kevin. She should have gone to work tonight, but needed to sort some things out.

She turned and walked to her living room hutch and picked up a picture of a man. She studied the inscription, "FOR 35 YEARS OF OUTSTANDING SERVICE TO THE NATIONAL SECURITY AGENCY - SENIOR CRYPTOLOGY ANALYST GARY TAYLOR."

All she ever wanted to do is make her father proud, something she fought for in the shadow of the brother she never had. *Maybe her father was right,* she thought, law enforcement was no place for a woman. It was still a man's world.

* * * * *

Colombia stirred for the first time in more than three months.

He was in a room one wing over from the University Medical Center ICU. It was a more secure room set up at the hospital to treat and hold criminals waiting trial. The FBI, DEA and D.C. police were always eager to take custody of a criminal as soon as possible. In Colombia's case, the FBI waited eagerly for a call that Colombia was out of his coma.

Disoriented, he jumped up and pulled the IV's and vitals sensors out, sending the alarms into overdrive.

Moments later, a nurse stood at Colombia's bedside keying information on his status into a computer terminal. She was updating Colombia's medical chart, "PATIENT: GARCIA, RODRIGUEZ 10:32 a.m. – awake, hungry, vitals normal."

* * * * *

Meanwhile, at the same time, Hazze sat at his computer screen. He had been monitoring

Colombia's medical condition for the past three months for Big D.

Hazze was looking at the exact same computer screen the nurse was looking at; only he was located at his office at International Antiques. He leaned in and watched as each keystroke flashed up on his computer screen.

* * * * *

Big D was pitching another business deal on the phone when Hazze burst in smiling. Big D stopped mid-sentence and covered the phone receiver. He looked at Hazze and muttered, "Goddamn Hackers!" *Give these computer geeks an office, some money and a bit of responsibility and they think they're God,* he thought to himself. He needed to finish this call, and then he would deal with Hazze.

He refocused back on his telephone conversation. It was a good thing it was a well-rehearsed pitch. He picked up right where he had left off.

"We acquire and sell information that has intrinsic value. Kinda like boutique information brokers." He continued to listen on the phone. And then a smile appeared, "Yep," Big D said, "secret agents." He laughed, and then hung up.

"I think you need to see this," Hazze said as he handed Big D a report.

Big D studied the report, and then smiled. Hazze was right; he would let him off the hook this time.

"Does Steelie know Colombia's awake?" Big D asked.

Hazze shook his head no and started for the door.

"Let's keep it that way," Big D said. "And Hazze, disable the hospital security cameras."

Big D watched Hazze open the door. He had one last order for his in-house hacker. "Oh, and Hazze," he said as Hazze turned around. "Next time knock and listen for me to say come in."

Hazze gave a quick nod and stood at the door, waiting for Big D's next command.

Big D grabbed the phone and dialed.

"Big D, what can I do for you?" a man said on the other end of the phone line.

Big D looked at Hazze. He was standing at the door like a dog waiting for his next command. Big D smiled at Hazze. He was learning. He made Hazze hold that pose for a few more seconds and then nodded to Hazze –he could leave.

Big D waited until Hazze closed the door.

"Time to prove you've got what it takes to work for me," Big D said into the phone receiver. He pulled his desk drawer open and whipped out a badge. He paused for a moment, and then flipped it open. It was Special Agent Jensen's FBI badge. Time was of the essence so he already had Hazze switch out Agent Jensen's photo for the new contract hit man's photo. The plan had always been that the moment Big D learned that Colombia's prognosis had improved and that he might be able to talk, he would put the contract hit out.

* * * * *

FBI Agent Larson watched as Agent Wells studied the whiteboard mapping out the details of the Albright murder. They were still running into brick walls at every turn. It was possible that Diggs was at the gravel pit the night Julia was killed. They only learned about the Diggs' connection to Steelie after he was killed. And the DEA were able to confirm the information through their Central America contacts. The only suspect they had in custody was still in a coma.

It also appeared "someone *could* have played" and "did play" Kevin Albright—some sort of vendetta given the business he was in. Larson wanted to turn *that could have played* into *did play Kevin Albright*. The barricade angle was going nowhere. The county highways department confirmed they had not erected the barricade signs Kevin claimed were there. However, the possibility that someone had put the barricade up and then took it down did exist, as did the possibility it was a prankster.

The XT's electronic malfunction held more promise. It could have been a NaviGator operator error, but with the NaviGator employee's disappearance, it looked intentional. They still needed to locate the former NaviGator employee and have a chat. To date, a check of her bank accounts indicated no large sums of money had been deposited or withdrawn.

On the Jensen-Murray angle, they were spending another day trying to construct new leads from the information they had—by studying yet another sketch of the crime scene. The names of the witnesses who were closest to seeing everything were clearly visible, "MURRAY" and "JENSEN." It was clear to Larson that Murray and Jensen should already be in jail. However, it was a two-edged sword. Now, they were heroes in the PR campaign to create a more positive image for the FBI and the war on drugs. Once they were arrested, the FBI's image would be in the toilet and the war on drugs being waged would be under intense scrutiny. It was important that they collect more evidence if they wanted to arrest Murray and Jensen, and fight the uphill battle against the bureaucracy, the courts and public opinion, ensuring the charges stick. Political fallout would be a completely separate issue—beyond their pay grade.

The telephone rang and Larson picked it up, "Special Agent Larson."

"Mr. Garcia is awake," the nurse said.

Larson smiled as he hung up the phone. This could be the big break they had been waiting for. It could crack the case wide-open. Maybe now they could get the evidence necessary to arrest Murray and Jensen. He motioned to Wells and said, "Frank, he's awake."

* * * * *

Special Agents Wells and Larson hurried past a doctor on his way out of Colombia's room. A pool of blood had collected under a chair located outside of Colombia's room.

A nurse looked up to see Wells and Larson approach. They flashed their badges.

She shook her head as she pulled a sheet over Colombia's body.

"What happened?" Larson said.

"Apparently, some guy walked in flashing an FBI badge," the nurse said. "Came up to the room, shot the guard at the door and walked in and shot Garcia."

"How's the guard?" Larson asked.

"He didn't make it," the nurse replied.

"Goddamn it!" Wells said. "How lucky can those bastards be?"

"Who else did you call?" Larson asked.

"Just the doctor in charge," the nurse replied.

Larson pushed for more information, "That's it? No one else?"

"That's it," the nurse said.

Larson surveyed the room as he mauled over the facts. The only people who knew that Colombia's status had changed were the doctor and the nurse. Then he looked at the bedside computer terminal. He stepped closer to the computer terminal. Rodriguez Garcia's electronic chart was displayed and the last comment on the screen read, "Time of death 1:05 p.m. Attending Physician Dr. Stevens."

Wells looked at computer monitor.

"Can you delete that?" he asked the nurse.

"These are official medical records," the nurse said.

Larson knew Wells would want to keep Colombia's death quiet, allowing them time to set some kind of trap for Jensen and Murray. He was already steps ahead.

"Where does that go?" Larson asked, pointing at a computer cable from the terminal, going to the wall outlet.

"The computer operations center," she said.

"Which floor?" Larson said.

"It's contracted out," she said. "Their offices are in the west end of the city."

Before Larson could pursue it any further, Wells nudged him, "Come on junior, no time to talk computer toys."

* * * * *

Larson had mapped out a plan. And the first chance he got, he headed back to his D.C. Field Office to execute it. He had already cleared it with Dr. Stevens. If his hunch played out, it would reveal that something suspicious was going on with the hospital's computers.

He composed an email to Dr. Stevens, the attending physician when Colombia had died. He took a few minutes to study it on his computer screen one last time. "To DrStevens@medcenter, From RaymondLarson@fbi, Rodriguez Garcia now cooperating on active file. Thanks for your intervention." It was a perfect piece of cheese for the trap.

He clicked the mouse activating SEND. His computer instantly chimed with a message on his screen, "Message opened."

Larson sat back and smiled to himself. Besides Dr. Stevens, he expected that one hungry mouse had also taken the cheese and soon he would catch the mouse in the bigger trap.

* * * * *

At the same time as Dr. Stevens opened and read the email from Agent Larson, Hazze also studied the same email. He had hacked into Dr. Stevens' email account as part of monitoring Colombia's medical status.

Hazze quickly printed off the email, grabbed it off the printer and started out of his office. Steelie appeared from out of nowhere and headed him off.

"Whoa there, Hazze. What's the rush?" Steelie asked.

Hazze handed Steelie the printout.

Steelie studied the printed email and put his arm around his best new friend Hazze.

"Let's not bother the big guy with this little item," Steelie said. "I think you and I can take care of this."

Steelie walked Hazze back into the Hacker's Office and sat him down at his computer.

CHAPTER 14

M EG HAD BARELY gotten back to her Fort Worth apartment when Palmer contacted her. He insisted, no, he demanded, that she turn around and return to Washington. What was so damn important that she had to personally come back and meet at the Department of Justice Special Investigation Unit's office in D.C.?

She stood at a window soaking up the warmth of sun's rays. She seemed to be looking for spiritual guidance from above a lot these days.

Meg glanced at her watch and turned to Investigator Burgess. As if harnessing the sun's rays, her eyes turned in to laser beams that burned right through him. She was on time and Palmer was late. *Damn men, always demanding, I want, I need—never giving or on time*, she thought as she waited for Palmer to show up.

Special Investigator Palmer burst in to the office and slapped two photos on the table. "Things are getting really interesting," he said.

Meg walked over to the table, picked up the photos and studied them.

"Who are these guys?" she asked.

"Special Agents Jensen and Murray," Palmer said. "The agents who claim they tried to save Mrs. Albright's life. It looks like they may have been up to a little moonlighting."

"What?" she said as she examined the photos closer.

"Yeah, they're potential suspects," Palmer said.

"Shit," Meg said as she threw the photos down on the table. She slowly sat down. Her anger at Palmer turned into total disbelief. "This may explain a few things," she said.

Palmer looked at Meg, waiting for her explanation.

"Kevin told me he called these guys," Meg said.

"What the hell was he thinking?" Palmer asked.

"He thought he was getting the run around from the Marshal's Office," Meg said. "And when he couldn't get through to Wells—" Meg stared at Burgess, expecting he would finish the sentence.

"He contacted Jensen," Burgess said.

"He knew Jensen lost a daughter to drugs. Said if you can't trust another grieving father, who can you trust?" Meg added.

"He's playing with us," Palmer said. "He knows what Jensen and Murray were up to."

"Big mistake," Burgess added.

Meg looked at Burgess, then Palmer.

"Really!" she said. "And running to please Martelli isn't?" She took a deep breath, "We've got to get him out of there."

"Are you thinking with your head," Palmer said, "or your heart?"

Meg was burning up on the inside. *Palmer and Burgess were no different than Joe Martelli. They were all out to fuel their egos and advance their personal careers and agendas*, she thought.

"I'm talking about an innocent human being that we're treating like a pawn on a chessboard," Meg said.

"Right," Palmer said, "and we're trying to move to checkmate and you're either in or out."

Exasperated, Meg jumped to her feet.

"This has nothing to do with saving innocent lives," she said. "This is all about serving your big—oh, just forget it." Meg stormed out, slamming the door behind her.

* * * * *

Special Agent Larson checked out the full moon through his windshield as he waited patiently in the FBI Washington Field Office parking lot. He had set the trap and now he just had to wait for things to play out.

The backdoor of the FBI Building opened and Agent Murray exited.

Larson crouched down in his vehicle as he watched Murray walk across the parking lot. Murray would not be able to hide from Larson this time. The full moon, the trap—it was all falling nicely into place. *Murray certainly looked like he was up to no good,* Larson thought. If he was trying to be inconspicuous, it was not working. He appeared nervous and hurried across the parking lot to his station wagon.

Moments later, Larson watched Murray's station wagon speed away. *Like shooting fish in a rain barrel,* Larson thought to himself as he started his car and followed.

* * * * *

Larson looked down into a deep pit and scrutinized the gravel bottom for signs of activity. The full moon lit the entire area down in the gravel pit up like floodlights on a crime scene investigation.

He had followed Murray out of the city and down several backcountry roads to get here. It had been several minutes since Murray turned on to a makeshift road, carved out by heavy hauler trucks carrying gravel out of the pit.

Larson watched Murray's station wagon roll to a stop.

As Murray stepped out of his station wagon, he wiped the sweat off his forehead.

Larson knew he had him cold, but he wanted to make Murray sweat just a little bit longer. He would let him nervously pace and impatiently survey the road for a party who would never arrive.

* * * * *

Murray pulled out his cell and dialed. It only rang once.

"Now what?" Agent Jensen said.

"At the pit waiting for Steelie. He's got information about Colombia," Murray said. He continued to pace and waited for Darrel Jensen to speak.

"Darrel?" Murray said.

"Get out of there—now!" Jensen said.

Murray hung up and ran for his station wagon.

* * * * *

Agent Larson drew his gun, his heart pounding. It would be his first major arrest, and it was a fellow FBI agent.

He was about to make his first big bust, and it would be a fellow FBI agent. He stormed over the hill.

"It's over, Murray," Larson yelled. There was no way he would dignify Murray by referring to him as a Special Agent.

"Put your hands in the air where I can see them."

Murray froze like a deer in the headlights and then slowly raised his hands.

CHAPTER 15

K EVIN PULLED HIS rental car up in front of Meg's apartment. She had called and suggested that maybe they could go to an AA meeting. It sounded like she certainly needed one. Personally, while he should be attending AA meetings to stay sober—given what he really felt—getting Julia's killers took precedence.

He gazed at the full moon as he waited—trying not to let his mind wander. But his mind quickly turned to thoughts of Julia and the last time they truly enjoyed an evening outdoors under a full moon. It had been a long time ago. He always seemed to be too busy at work on those full moon nights, even though they always enjoyed those special moments—the outdoors, the serenity. It was just the two of them snuggling under the stars and gazing at a full moon. Those must have been the moments Julia—Jewels—gathered her inspiration to paint and the courage to stay with him.

He would never erase the memory of the last time he and Jewels enjoyed the special moment Mother Nature gave them—it was a year ago. He, Julia and Sebastian went to the park to celebrate his AA anniversary. On their tenth wedding anniversary, it was only a matter of a day or two and they would have had another opportunity to enjoy a full moon. They had even talked about it earlier that night. Julia had joked she would believe it when she saw it. Kevin had booked the evening in his calendar, but it was too little, too late. Now every time he looked into the night sky and saw a full moon, he would think about Julia and what they had missed—because of him, and what they would never have—because of him. He shuddered as he thought about it and forced himself back into the moment.

Meg appeared from the apartment building and looked for a familiar vehicle.

Kevin noticed her searching for his car and honked the horn. In an effort to throw off any one who might be getting close to finding him, he had started switching rental cars every day or so. Tonight, he had another rental vehicle and he knew Meg would not recognize it.

* * * * *

Meg smiled. *But it seemed forced* Kevin thought.
"Looks like your day didn't go so well," he said as glanced in the rearview mirror. Then he looked at Meg. She was fussing with her jacket.

"It's been hellish to be exact," Meg said.

"Anything you want to talk about?" Kevin said as he glanced in the rearview mirror again. He was not sure but he thought a vehicle was following them.

"Did you ever have a day when you realized that the people you thought you knew are really not the people you thought they were?" Meg said.

Kevin was attentive to his rearview mirror and did not hear her.

"Josh. Kevin! Did you hear me?" Meg said.

"I think *I'm* being followed," Kevin said.

Meg turned in her seat and looked back through the rear window.

Kevin reached into the glove box and pulled out his .500 Magnum.

"I need to let you out," he said.

Meg eyed Kevin's .500 Magnum. She opened her purse and pulled out a gun.

Kevin exchanged a glance with Meg—she had some explaining to do.

Meg stared back through the rear window. The vehicle was getting closer.

"Step on it!" she said.

"Can you make them out?" Kevin asked.

Meg looked back again. The vehicle was almost on their bumper and she saw the driver.

"Jensen!" she said.

* * * * *

As Special Agent Jensen closed in on the rental car, he pulled his gun from the glove box.

* * * * *

Meg studied the approaching intersection and pointed, "Quick, take a left there." She glanced back again and noticed Jensen's gun pointed out the car window at them.

"Get down!" she said as she ducked.

Kevin stared straight ahead and stepped on the gas. He did not have time to think about ducking. He was going to confront the guy.

Shots rang out. A bullet smashed through their rear car window.

Kevin cranked the steering wheel hard left and drove down the street. He looked over at Meg as she raised her head above the seat and started to aim her gun.

She hesitated.

He would have to do this himself; she knew Jensen and he could not trust her or anyone in his life to help him—let alone kill someone. He had already killed once for Julia and he did not need to dance with the alcohol demon to give him the courage. This was about bypassing any sense of reason any sane person would have—in search of justice, in a world where nothing was making sense. It rationalized what he had done and what he was about to do.

He pushed the brake pedal to the mat. Their rental vehicle slid sideways down the street and screeched to a stop. In an instant, Kevin sprang out and waited for Jensen's vehicle to appear.

* * * * *

Kevin watched Jensen's vehicle squeal around the corner. He stared down the driver as the vehicle accelerated toward him.

Jensen was trying to drive with one hand and aim his gun out the window with the other.

Kevin could see the gun; it was pointed directly at him.

Kevin did not flinch. He lifted his gun, aimed and emptied the .500 Magnum into Jensen's vehicle and sent it crashing into two parked cars.

Meg rushed over to Kevin, "Are you OK?"

"Jensen!" Kevin said, "The FBI agent?" He glanced at Meg's gun, "You've got a gun!"

"I think we need to talk," Meg said.

Kevin waved his .500 Magnum as he paced.

"Yeah," he said. "This time I've got one of them cold." He looked at Meg, "Now we'll go to the police."

"Kevin, this is bigger," Meg looked away, then turned back and stepped closer to him. "This is real big," she said.

"Right, an FBI agent just tried to kill me and—" he said.

"Kevin—I work for the Justice Department. I'm a Special Investigator," Meg said.

"What?" Kevin said. "I don't believe this. It's, it's a bad dream. No, it's a fucking nightmare, and I can't get out of it." Kevin backed away from Meg.

Meg tried to step closer to him.

"Listen, I know you'll find it hard to believe anything I say now, but—"

Kevin backed away further—incensed.

"Here I am telling you that my wife was killed. I'm in the Witness Protection Program—you knew it all along."

"Kevin—" Meg tried to speak.

"Trying to catch my wife's killer—people are trying to kill me, in case you haven't noticed. Oh, but you're an undercover agent, that doesn't matter."

"Kevin, I—"

"Meg, if that is your name, well that, that AA thing, how can you do it!" Kevin's eyes avoided Meg's eyes and landed on her crotch. "At least my father had the balls to kill himself." He watched the tears roll down Meg's cheeks, but did not believe them for one minute.

Then he had a sudden realization, "The park—Covert Ops, who would say that? Damn it! I should've known."

Meg attempted to move closer to Kevin.

He pulled away.

"Now tears! Call Martelli! You know him right?" He tossed the .500 Magnum at Meg's feet, "I'm sure he's at least capable of taking care of this."

Kevin turned his back on Meg and walked to his car.

"I know this won't help now," Meg yelled, "but, when I told you I had something I had to do, well, I was trying to get this whole crazy thing stopped."

Kevin turned to Meg, "Lucky for me that your people are incompetent, or I'd be dead. Tell Martelli he's toast—I'm in charge now!" Kevin opened the car door, jumped in and slammed it shut. Punching the accelerator, he forced a squeal out of the rental car's front tires.

Meg yelled to Kevin as he drove away, "I couldn't, so I'm resigning—just wanted to let you know."

CHAPTER 16

THE FBI INTERROGATION room was hot tonight—one of many strategies used to make those being interviewed break. Only this time, Larson cranked the heat up to eighty-five degrees and there was no water for Murray to drink as he contemplated his next lie. As fast as Special Agent Murray pulled paper tissues out of the box and wiped his face, more sweat poured out. His stomach rumbled like a man with Montezuma's revenge with no place to run to. He would break soon or his insides would be sucked out his asshole. At least that was Larson's plan.

Special Agent Larson looked at Special Agent Wells. He had become more like a partner, particularly in the last couple of hours. While Agent Larson was still piecing together all the details, he had identified a major security breach with hospital computer systems and capitalized on it. University Medical Center had contracted out data center services to the private sector and it turned out the company providing the services was under extreme financial pressures and on the verge of filing for bankruptcy protection.

Special Agent Wells had even agreed to follow Larson's lead in playing out the "good guy—bad guy" tag team as they interrogated Murray. The drill would have them pacing around Murray as he sat at a table in the interrogation room. Swooping in like vultures, they would take turns picking Murray apart.

Murray sat with his hands clasped and stared at the floor, except when the probing got hot, and he could not contain the sweat—his body telegraphed the stress, distress, and panic.

"Tell us how you ended up at the Albright murder scene *again?*" Wells asked as he swooped in again.

"I was following up on a tip," Murray said.

It was a long shot, but Larson still had not located the former NaviGator operator for questioning about the circumstances surrounding Kevin Albright's XT electrical failure. Maybe Murray had more information about that night that he was not sharing.

"Did you have anything to do with putting up a barricade that night?" Larson asked.

"What barricade?" Murray said.

"The one that was supposed to keep people from driving to the gravel pit—you know the pit where the drug deal was going down?" Larson said.

"I don't know what you're talking about," Murray said.

"Did you have anything to do with a NaviGator operator tampering with Mr. Albright's onboard electronics system?" Larson asked.

"What?" Murray responded.

"Do you know where we might find her?" Larson probed.

"I don't know what you are taking about," Murray responded.

Larson had heard enough—it was time to go in for the kill.

"So just to confirm it then," Larson said, "you were out there following up on a tip."

"That's correct," Murray said.

Larson flipped a piece of paper on the table. He was sure this would push Murray over the cliff. Murray would have no choice but to cough up all the evidence they needed.

"So this tip, was it this email from International Antiques?" Larson said.

Murray looked at Larson for the first time, "I want to speak to a lawyer."

* * * * *

Kevin drove his rental car on a downtown street. It was as if he was cruising for the perfect *woman.* Tonight the woman was scotch, Johnnie Walker Blue Label to be precise, and he knew he would find her at a bar. Tonight he would loose his AA virginity, barely past his third AA birthday. How did he get here, a downtown street at night? It was the last of his feeble attempts to talk himself out of taking a drink. He knew exactly how he got there—his choice, his decision.

He had played the "how did he get here," tape a lot lately, almost as much as when he first got sober. Daily, hourly and even minute-by-minute, he would ask, "How did I get here?" Three years ago, it helped him fight off the demons to stay sober. Now, every time he asked the question it pulled him closer to giving in to the lady—drinking up her liquids. It was all part of the setup to relapse. In AA, they told him that taking the first drink started days and weeks before someone actually relapsed.

A car horn honked. Kevin snapped back into the moment just as the traffic light turned red. He nearly rear-ended a car in front of him as it screeched to a stop.

As he sat at the red light, he played his time at Logic Computer Services over and over in his head: how he met Meg at an AA meeting, obviously it was not luck or fate. She looked so much like Julia. Maybe that really was coincidence or maybe it was part of the bigger plan too.

Then he thought about the hackers he was chasing and Julia's killers. Maybe they weren't the most dangerous people in on the planet. He was beginning to believe Joe Martelli was even more dangerous, a hotshot executive assistant working for the top man in the United States justice system. Kevin wanted to believe the Attorney General did not know what was happening in his own backyard. If he did, the justice system—the government, had serious problems that would destroy the most powerful country in the world. Even if the Attorney General didn't know, the outcome would still be the same—devastating.

A power tripping Executive Assistant, or perhaps he was on the take—maybe he didn't want to involve NIPC because he was being well paid to work for the hackers or killers. What about the bad FBI agents? Or Meg? He wanted to believe she was not bad, but who screws over a man who has lost his wife? She worked for the Justice Department and ultimately reported to the Attorney General. This all could not be happening to him by coincidence, and without the Attorney General knowing anything.

* * * * *

Kevin heard a familiar tune playing—it was a Bryan Adams favorite. He had danced to it with Julia at their wedding anniversary. He slowly turned. The music was coming from a bar. A big window sign flashed, "HAPPY HOUR ALL-DAY."

Coincidence, fate or divine intervention—it took hold of Kevin.

The traffic light turned green. The honk of a vehicle behind him brought him back to the moment for the second time. He was on a busy street and needed to drive. He turned away from the bar window sign and stared into the intersection. Another honk. He fought the urge to pull into the nearest parking stall, but the flashing bar sign beckoned him; he turned to look at it one more time. Another honk, he glanced in his rearview mirror. *Go or park*, Kevin thought, as his mind raced and he fought Pavlov's law. He was already drooling on the inside and he realized he was just like a primeval animal drooling over a steak bone.

* * * * *

Kevin sat at the bar counter, like a starving dog waiting for his bowl of kibbles. He was defeated. The alcohol demon had won. Now she would get her reward—have her way with him. He would drink the contents of her vial.

The bartender flipped a glass up on the counter in front of Kevin.

Kevin licked his dry lips as he watched the bartender drop ice into the glass. The clink of ice hitting the glass bottom echoed in his head. He swallowed hard.

"What'll it be?" the bartender asked.

Kevin looked past the bartender at a face in the mirror. It was a man about to betray a promise to his wife. He turned away.

"Excuse me, sir—" the bartender said.

Kevin's leg pumped up and down on the bar rest.

"Johnnie Walker Blue Label," he blurted out. Drinking beer was like taking the long way to get home when you knew a shortcut, and a rum and coke did little to accelerate the feeling he wanted. A long pour Blue Label straight up was the closest he would ever get to mainlining his medication of choice. He glanced up at the mirror. The image he saw again pulled him in. Damn it, he could not hide from himself. Everywhere he looked, there he was.

"Make it a double," he said.

The bartender splashed scotch over the ice.

Kevin stared at the ice as it responded, cracking with bubbles rising in the scotch. The ice dancing in the scotch was mesmerizing. He turned away and looked into the mirror.

The bartender noticed a look of anguish on Kevin's face as he stared at his mirror image.

The clank of the bartender setting the glass on the counter broke the moment.

Kevin turned away. He could not look the bartender in the eye, as he was sure he looked like an underage minor who knew he was in the wrong place.

"Rough night?" the bartender said.

"You could say that," Kevin said as he pulled a roll of bills out of his pocket. "What's the damage?"

"Three ninety-five," the bartender said.

Kevin was surprised, "Three ninety-five."

The bartender motioned toward the window sign, "HAPPY HOUR ALL-DAY."

"Cheap booze all day," he said.

Kevin dropped a pile of bills on the bar counter and grabbed the drink. He looked into the glass. Captivated by the contents, he swished the ice around. His eyes blinked several times as he tried to focus.

A drunken man's voice played in his head, "You want to be a computer programmer like your old man? Forget it. And don't ever think about a family—you'll disappoint them. You'll die alone just like me."

"I'll never be a father like you!" Kevin said, as he raised the drink glass to his mouth. He swallowed to make room for the drink.

He looked into the mirror and heard Julia's voice, "You have to choose to drink or not."

He swished the drink harder and heard Meg's voice, "You know crazy thinking—did you ever think he got frustrated at not being able to get sober? Maybe he thought his only choices were to drink and hurt you more or just end it so you could move on as a family."

Kevin raised the glass to his mouth and inhaled the scotch aroma. He looked at the man's face in the mirror.

"You're not your father," Julia's voice played in his head. "You won't abandon your family."

Kevin sat the glass down on the bar counter. The demon inside him pleaded with him—she wanted him to pick her up. His head started spinning. *Pick it up. Put it down,* the voices argued back and forth, faster and louder.

"Fake it until you make it," played in his head. That is what he told himself the night Julia was killed.

So was he a fake-it guy, or a make-it guy?

Enough, Kevin thought. He vomited out the words, "I'll never die like you, dad!"

He picked the glass up and hurled it at his image in the mirror. The contents exploded and the mirror shattered, sending glass and ice everywhere. He knew his father committed suicide. And he knew that if he took the drink he would be doing the same thing—maybe not with a gun, but the end result would certainly be the same.

Kevin stared at the scotch running down the wall—half of his face reflecting back in a piece of mirror that had not shattered. Ironically, that is exactly who Kevin was when he drank, half the man he was when he was sober. Kevin looked at the bartender.

As if the bartender was a recovering alcoholic who felt his pain, he was not overly surprised. Kevin nodded to the pile of bills on the counter, "Keep it."

The bartender nodded.

Kevin stepped off the bar stool and ran out of the bar before he could change his mind again.

* * * * *

Big D stared out his office window at the city nightscape. The drug business in Central America he operated was looking so much more appealing than information brokering. He on the phone and could hear what sounded like a fighter jet engines firing up their engines.

"What the hell's going on?" Big D said.

* * * * *

At the same time, the I Man watched three Chinese manufactured SF-X14 stealth fighter jet prototypes fire up and taxi to a runway on a Kazakhstan airstrip. He was trying to talk on his cell phone over the roar of the jet engines, "I'm at a Kazakhstan airstrip." With the cell tightly pressed to his left ear, he covered his right ear with his free hand as the jet engine burners kicked in.

"It's time to go hunting," the I Man said.

"Contractor's onboard," Big D said. "He'll open an email from you, and it'll launch a program, find *your* two-hundred thousand sensors and give you complete control."

"The money's wired to a holding account," the I Man said. "It will be released when I see the package."

"I'll email the package to your International Antiques email account," Big D said as he smiled; he was somewhat relieved. "Once I see the cash, you'll get the contractor's email address."

The I Man grinned. "The cyber hunter's magic bullet," he said as he watched an SF-X14 approach. "You got to see these things to believe them, Mach 3 plus. I could be in Washington in three hours."

The SF-X14 passed over with a loud boom just as it broke the sound barrier. It reverberated through his cell phone.

* * * * *

Big D held the phone away from his ear, and mumbled to himself, "No more contracts."

* * * * *

Kevin stared at the hole in the motel room wall that once was a telephone outlet. It had become a sort of focal meditation point. In the digital world, it was the access point to the world. Tonight, as his mind raced, he wondered who would even use landlines these days. He was vigilant every minute now. It was after midnight, demon time. And it was no time for "fake-it" if he didn't want the alcohol demons to seize control of his mind again. He needed to fill his mind with work, so much work that not even a hairline fracture of an opening existed.

He plugged a USB wireless modem into his laptop and quickly got his mini-hacking application operating and input a series of commands. Using these advanced settings, he started the application to start scanning messages.

* * * * *

Kevin studied an email message on his laptop screen. It read "DECRYPTED MESSAGE: To: I MAN, Subject: Pipe Cleaner. 200 T Pipe Cleaner package attached. Upon payment confirmation, contractor address will be provided. Hazze."

Kevin stroked Sebastian's chin as he studied the message.

"Pipe cleaners?" he said.

He looked at Sebastian. Sebastian's puzzled look mirrored the puzzle challenging Kevin's brain as he leaned back, in deep thought. He stared at the ceiling, then back at the laptop.

Kevin clicked on "200 T PIPE CLEANER PACKAGE" attachment. The screen went black, and then flashed, "SEARCHING FOR PIPELINE SWITCHES NETWORK CONNECTION." He pulled in closer to the screen as it flashed, "You are not connected to local network. Please retry."

Kevin's eyes widened. "Holy Shit," he said. He had seen these digital RATS before. Some were really cyber "bombs," and this one certainly fit that bill. One critical piece of information was all that was needed to light the fuse—the contractor's address—in this case. He suspected it was an email address. And once the I Man got the contractors email address, he would send the email to the contractor. Like other digital RATs, the email would bypass the firewalls. And once opened, this RAT would search for pipeline switch controllers on the inside.

CHAPTER 17

K EVIN SAT AT a creaky table in his motel room. His fingers danced across the keyboard as the table wobbled to the keystroke rhythm he had established. He paused and waited for his laptop to respond. The Internet home page for "HELMES AND ASSOCIATES" flashed up. Wayne had already done the prudent thing, filing to rename the company. The tax implications on a go-forward basis would be simpler and he understood how difficult it would be for Wayne to continue referring to the company as Albright and Helmes.

Kevin hastily keyed in his user ID and password and waited to access to his old hacking tools used to catch "black hats"—the bad hackers. A response flashed up on the screen, "Access Denied."

"Shit," Kevin said as he thumped the table and stared at the computer. *What did you expect?* he thought. *Wayne's a security professional and you knew he would eventually deactivate your account—you died, right?* He needed those tools now with even more reason now. He had avoided drawing his partner and friend into this nightmare, but now he was pushed—in a corner—a place where desperate measures were required. If he did not act, the attack being orchestrated would most likely kill Wayne and his family in any event. Kevin jumped up, grabbed his cell phone and dialed.

* * * * *

142 | DEADLY INVISIBLE ENEMIES: BOOK 2

Wayne coddled his newborn baby as he waited for the baby bottle to warm. The phone rang. He adjusted his little baby girl to grab the phone before it rang again.

"Hello," he said in a low voice. He could hear someone breathing on the other end of the line. "Hello," he said again. He glanced at the baby bottle and was about to hang up.

Kevin tried to speak, but the words were not coming out. Then in the silence he sensed Wayne was about to hang up.

"Don't hang up," Kevin blurted out. "It's—"

"Who is this?" Wayne said.

Kevin heard a baby start to cry in the background, "It's me—"

Wayne snapped to attention just as Christy walked into the kitchen.

"Kevin!" Wayne said.

Christy froze, and then the baby went into full out scream mode. She quickly took the baby and rushed to grab the nearest cordless phone to listen in.

"I'm sorry, Wayne," Kevin said, as he heard the baby cry louder.

"Kevin?" Christy said.

"You had the baby?" Kevin said.

"Six pounds, two ounces," Christy replied, "Julia Louise Helmes." She dropped the phone to attend to baby.

Kevin searched for words. They had named their baby after Jewels. Moved and torn—he was guilt ridden over what he had put them through; yet his heart warmed on the inside about how they had honored Julia. He believed they were probably still alive because of the distance he had put between himself and Wayne.

"Thanks for everything," Kevin said. "I visited Jewels—Josh. I wanted to contact you—didn't want to put your family in jeopardy. But now," he took a deep breath, "I think you and half the east coast are in danger—any one near an oil or gas pipeline."

"What?" Wayne said.

"It's been a bit of a nightmare," Kevin said. "There are people hunting for me. People who killed Julia."

Wayne looked over at Christy as she fed the baby.

"I should've been all over Martelli," Kevin said. "Maybe Julia would still be alive."

"What do you mean?" Wayne said without waiting for Kevin to respond he immediately asked, "Where are you?"

"Was in the Witness Protection Program" Kevin said. "Now I'm living off the grid! Martelli thinks he's pulling the strings—they're on my turf now!"

"Kevin—" Wayne said.

"Wayne, the less you know—"

"What are you into, Kevin?"

"Staying alive, getting Julia's killers—stopping a pipe bomber.'

"Pipe bomber," Wayne said, glancing at his wife.

Christy's eyes opened wide as she fed the baby.

"We've got a digital RAT about to inhabit a network controlling oil and gas pipeline infrastructure. I need to get access to the computer programs we used on the East Coast Power Corp project," Kevin said.

"It was you!" Wayne said. "You accessed our files. We set a trap to get the hacker who accessed our files. You just tried again to access our files. It triggered a silent alert."

"At least one security system works," Kevin said. He took another deep breath, "I've got to shut down International Antiques."

"Who?" Wayne asked.

Kevin knew anyone trying to trace and find him would be closing in on his cell phone call. He needed to get off his cell immediately, if he wanted to protect Wayne and his family.

"Gotta run," Kevin said. "Enable my last password."

"Kevin. Kevin!" Wayne heard a click. The line went dead.

* * * * *

NIPC Director James Bullock surveyed the Main Operations Command Center. It was large, expensive and jammed with banks of computer consoles staffed with the best and brightest men and women from across the United States. Given the threat cyberspace posed to the globe, they even had staff from other countries including the United Kingdom. Like fighting a world outbreak of a new pandemic, they were fighting a cyber virus that was growing stronger and more deadly with each day and night that passed. Everyone was equipped with wireless headsets. Their bloodshot bug-eyes stared at computers as they scrutinized millions of lines of data traffic flashing across their screens. This was a Herculean task and the eyes-on approach was fundamental to detecting suspicious traffic.

James glanced at his watch and then surveyed the floor again—the massive investment in money, talent and equipment for which the President had pushed hard needed to prove its worth. He looked at his watch again as he stood behind Matt at his console, waiting for Matt to get off the phone.

Matt hung up and spun around.

"Sorry sir, we're still trying to source their encryption program."

"Give me something—anything!" James Bullock demanded. "I've got to brief the President and N.S.C. in three hours."

A female NIPC analyst with a British accent ran up to Matt's desk.

"Moscow Desk has advised computer chatter's stopped," she said.

"Damn it," Matt said as he looked at James. "We were hoping we might intercept a digital key or something—anything that might help crack the encryption code."

"President's not going to be happy," James said, as he looked around the office.

"Code's not one that has been developed in the U.S.," Matt said, "at least not by our contractors or partners—military or civilian."

James was feeling the effect of a long night and he could see that Matt was too as he watched Matt stand. He was stiff and tried to stretch his muscles. James knew he needed to push his analysts hard now. The stakes were too high.

"President gets us a fifty billion dollar budget to defend the country in cyberspace," James said. "All I can tell him is we know that someone is doing something—we just don't know who *they* are, what they are doing, or who they are doing it to."

"Kinda like they're giving us the bird," the female NIPC analyst said, "but we can't see them."

James glanced at Matt, and then at the NIPC analyst. She was right, but he tried to ignore her as it only fueled his anger. He turned back to Matt and asked, "So what else have you got Matt?"

"What about the Blackstone angle?" Matt said.

"Right," James replied, growing more frustrated. "I'll tell the President we suspect Blackstone is involved—just the ammunition our *friendly vultures* are waiting for. They'd swoop in, in a nanosecond, and end the NIPC 'experiment' I don't think so."

CHAPTER 18

S PECIAL AGENT LARSON walked down the long hall toward the D.C. Field Office Interrogation Room. He stopped at the door and waited for Special Agent Wells to catch up so they could enter together. Larson's tech savvy had moved his "street creds" way up on the bosses' radar after he blew the Jensen-Murray investigation wide open.

* * * * *

L arson looked at the once infamous PR agents for the FBI—Murray and Jensen. Now they were just sad, pathetic individuals trying to avoid jail time. Bruised and bandaged, they were a disgrace to the FBI, unworthy of the chairs and table they sat at. He quickly turned to his partner, trying not to give them any more of his attention than necessary.

"Gentlemen, my partner, Special Agent Larson," Wells said as he looked at Larson. "The lead agent on this case has managed to cut a deal with the Attorney General's office."

"In return for your cooperation," Larson said, "you will be placed in the Federal Witness Protection Program."

Larson watched Jensen look at Murray, his eyes narrowed in disgust. *What a twisted bit of justice*, Larson thought. Two men helping to dust protected witnesses were going into the program. He was disappointed that Murray and Jensen offered little help in trying to piece together the NaviGator angle.

"We found the former NaviGator employee," Larson said, hoping to get a rise out of Murray or Jensen.

"What's that got to do with us?" Jensen said.

"I don't know yet," Larson said. "Unfortunately she's dead, apparently she committed suicide—"

"Go figure," Wells said. "She could have fingered you and she's gone. How convenient."

"We don't know what you're talking about," Murray said.

"But you'll cooperate on what you do know about the leaked files—right Murray?" Wells said.

Murray nodded in agreement.

Larson looked at Jensen, "Cooperation—evidence in return for Wit Pro. Is that clear?"

Jensen's face hardened as his hands turned into clenched fists.

"My partner asked if that was clear, Jensen," Wells said.

"Clear," Jensen said. He turned to Murray, "I swear, I'll—."

"Let it go Jensen," Larson said. "It's time to do your daughter's memory a little justice."

"You'll be in the perfect place," Wells said, as he approached Jensen and pushed his nose into Jensen's face. "There are people who'd like to see you dead."

Larson noticed Wells crack a smile. Wells was relishing every second. He knew Jensen and Murray were getting what they deserved, but he knew he would have to keep a close eye on his partner. There was no room for personal agendas in law enforcement. In time, he hoped Wells would realize that too.

* * * * *

The Situation Room at the White House was full of caffeine charged military brass and senior advisers; all hunkered down around a large boardroom table. The room had been getting hotter by the minute driving everyone to remove their jackets, roll up their sleeves and loosen their ties.

The CIA Director looked around the table and then delivered the CIA's assessment of the situation. "Our Moscow INTEL indicates the Kazakhstan computer installation is not sophisticated enough to pose a threat to national security."

The President turned to Attorney General Robert Waters. Waters nodded to the NIPC Director, James Bullock.

James knew the President and Attorney General were looking for something credible from NIPC. To date, all the President had gotten was a lot of flack for money spent on some notion that cyber warfare posed a major threat to national security.

"We're trying to crack the code to the traffic we've intercepted." James said.

"I gave you all the resources you asked for—all that fancy equipment. Billions spent on computer security and intelligence and *you* can't read an email," the President said.

James knew the comment was coming and it was fair game for NIPC—him in particular, as he personally committed to the President to establish a world-class computer intelligence organization. The caveat was it would take money and talent. The President gave him the financial resources and a free rein to reach into any U.S. government agency, go overseas, or contract with the private sector to get the people he needed.

"Mr. President," the Chairman Joint Chiefs of Staff said. "I think we need to put our east-coast military on full alert. We have twenty-six nuclear facilities, four liquefied natural gas terminals and major high-density population targets—New York, Philadelphia, Boston, Washington—"

"I need more time," James said as he watched the President stand and pace. He wished he could give the President something, anything, to avoid military intervention or more meddling by the CIA. They were both trying to score points. For the CIA, scoring a win with the President would translate into support for more funding for overseas operations, for NIPC, a win would give the President the ammunition he needed to save NIPC from elimination. James was in the twilight of his career and tired of fighting wars of political gamesmanship. He had a job to do and that meant being fully honest.

"And what do we tell our citizens?" the President said. "That based on some email communications that we think originated in Russia—"

"Or Pakistan or Iraq—" James added.

"Or the U.S. for that matter!" the CIA Director quipped.

James could see that the President was displeased with the interruptions and that the President wanted to finish his thought, while he paced the room.

"As I started to say, based on some email communications that we think originated in .Russia." The President looked at James, "or Iraq—Pakistan," and then at the CIA Director. "Or our own damn country—maybe we should add North Korea—we believe there is a serious threat to our national security."

The President stopped pacing, and rested his clenched fists on the table. He scanned the group, stopping at the Chairman Joint Chiefs of Staff.

"We tell them nothing, Mr. President," the Chairman said. "It's just a routine military training exercise."

James watched the President slowly pan the table. The President had to act and it was unlikely the President would give him more time. The unspoken words in the room— 9/11, Pearl Harbor—were single target strikes. They paled in comparison to a cyber attack hitting multiple targets simultaneously. Not just one nuclear facility. But all twenty-six facilities at the same time. No visible aircraft. No physical presence—just an invisible flash of zeros and ones pulsing through the air toward its target. Not being able to decipher and action email transmissions was like not comprehending and acting on Japanese warplane sighting reports before Pearl Harbor was attacked. James knew this was the President's silent poll for final suggestions and at the moment, he didn't have anything more he could add. He would just have to wait for the decision.

"Start your training exercise," the President said.

"Right away, sir," the Chairman said.

"Mr. President—" James said, and quickly bit his tongue. *Damn it,* James thought. His ego was getting in the way. He was failing on his commitment to the President. What did he hope to gain by opening his mouth? Stalling to buy time was not a solution. A team player would recognize that the President had no choice but to prepare for a major—no, a catastrophic event. He braced himself for what was about to come.

The President zeroed in on James, "You heard the Chief. We've got major targets—over a hundred million American citizens live in east-coast states, hell, New York City alone is a nine-thousand square mile target, fifty million citizens! Until you can give me something more concrete to go on, the way I see it, we train and pray it doesn't become more."

The President headed for the door, paused and turned to the CIA Director, "Have your operatives got any more INTEL on the potential threat to our oil coming out of Canada?"

The CIA Director gave a quick nod no, "We think a bigger threat on the energy file lies in China. The Chinese President is very displeased with your embargo on our energy technology exports to his country. We're attempting to validate some Internet chatter involving a rogue operative called the I Man."

"Is it possible they are using the Internet to spread propaganda—to advance their cause?" the President asked.

"That's a good question, Mr. President," James said, "and a very real challenge. Even if we have the code to decrypt transmissions, we must still sift through millions of messages to identify real potential threats."

"Based on my experience, propaganda is a tactic intended to deflect our attention away from the real target—the east-coast in this case," the Chairman added.

Everyone stood as the President exited the room. The sound of a door slamming reverberated around the room.

The Chairman flashed a smile at James, adding more fuel to the fire that was smoldering deep inside James. The *vultures* were circling. *That bastard*, James thought, *just castrated me in front of the President.* He would not forget this moment, but as he tried to calm down, he reminded himself he was also a team player and would do whatever it took to support the President.

* * * * *

A laptop cursor flashed. Kevin's eyes appeared to blink in-sync with the cursor as he stared at it. Suddenly, his laptop blasted out a status report on the screen, "ALBRIGHT NETWORK PACK OPERATIONAL - Searching for Pipe Cleaner Traffic."

Kevin stood and walked to the motel room window and cracked the curtain. It was dark, but Kevin could make out the nighttime silhouette of a prostitute escorting her latest John to a room.

He turned back to his laptop screen and hoped that tonight he would find the key to unlock the latest flurry of Internet traffic he had intercepted. A message flashed up on his screen, "I Man; Subject: Pipe Cleaner Encrypt Source Code UPDATE. Hazze, International Antiques."

Kevin ran to his laptop. He studied the subject line and said, "Encrypt Source Code updated." If his suspicions were right, a new encryption code for email and other computer-based communications was being put into play. NIPC could use it to read emails and any other digital transmissions they intercepted. He took a deep breath and opened his copy of the intercepted email. His eyes lit up.

"Bingo," he said to himself. He grabbed his cell phone and punched in a number. He prayed he would be able to talk to someone at NIPC who knew him.

"National Infrastructure Protection Center Desk," Matt said.

"Matt?" Kevin said.

"Who is this?" Matt replied.

"Someone who's going to save your bacon," Kevin said.

"Kevin?" Matt said, "Kevin Albright?"

"I've just intercepted an encryption software transmission," Kevin said. "My guess is it's likely the software you're looking for."

"Kevin," Matt said, "I'll need to verify—"

"Gotta go. Contact Wayne Helmes," Kevin hung up and looked at Sebastian. "Let's see what else we caught."

CHAPTER 19

MATT STOOD AT his upper deck workstation overlooking the NIPC Main Ops Center. He stared down at the staff—telephone lines and workstations buzzed with activity. He had a phone glued to his ear.

His computer beeped, prompting him that he had an email. Matt glanced at the message that had appeared on screen, "You Have Mail From Wayne Helmes."

"Got it, Wayne," Matt said. He hung up and breathed a sigh of relief. He glanced over at the NIPC analyst's workstation ten feet from his workstation. She was studying email traffic scooped up in the last hour. He abruptly walked to her workstation.

"We got it," he said. "We got the damn Russian transmission."

"Gotta have the encryption software," she said in her English accent, nodding to an indecipherable email on her computer screen, "if we hope to break the code—actually read this stuff."

"That's right," Matt said. "And that's exactly what we got. The updated release of their encryption software source code."

She jumped out of her chair, pumped her fist and did a happy dance—throwing an invisible ball into the ground—as if she had just scored a touchdown.

It was a major breakthrough. Matt even found a reason to crack a joke. "Is that your impression of a football touchdown celebration?"

"Rugby," she said trying to pull back her enthusiasm. "They've just given us the keys to everything," she said. "They won't know what hit them," she added as she picked up her phone; speed dialed and handed it to Matt.

* * * * *

James woke to what seemed to have become a nightly ritual. One, maybe two hours of sleep only to be interrupted by a phone call from the NIPC Ops Center. He glanced over at the clock; it was 3:35 a.m. Tonight, he almost got three hours sleep and would be up in little more than an hour. Surely, they could have waited. He grabbed the phone.

"Sir, we've got it," Matt said. "We've got them."

"Do you know what time it is?" James said, trying to get the synaptic connections in his brain firing—like waking a computer up from a sleep state. "Got what? Got who?"

"Kevin Albright's alive!" Matt said, "He's intercepted a motherlode communication, Russian we think. It's the new release of their encryption software. We've got their playbook."

James' synaptic connections kicked into overdrive. Any grogginess that may have existed vanished in a split-second. "I'm on my way," James said.

* * * * *

Kevin glanced out the motel window—he had pulled another all-nighter and the sun was just rising. He walked back to his laptop, studied an email and turned deadly serious. "Terminate IA agreement with LCS tonight." His window to get Julia's killers was closing. LCS was about to be terminated by International Antiques, and the threat of potential mass destruction was growing every minute Internet traffic continued to flow between International Antiques and rogue operatives. He reached for his phone.

* * * * *

Wayne's office phone rang and he picked up, "Helmes and Associates."

"I need to get into Logic Computer Services tonight," Kevin said, "before they blow the place up."

"Kevin," Wayne said as he sat up in his chair. "You've got them—Jensen and Murray! They're cooperating. You can stop chasing Julia's killers. The FBI are on it."

Kevin had seen too much—been through too much and did not trust anyone to get Julia's killers, certainly not the FBI.

"Come on home," Wayne said.

Kevin only thought about it for a millisecond. His closest friend and his family, a new baby, and thousands of innocent lives would be lost if someone did not stop these guys.

"There won't be a home to go to if I don't stop these guys," Kevin said.

"Kevin—"

"Wayne," Kevin interrupted, "when I'm finished with Carlos Steelie's clients, he'll experience his worst nightmare—to be ruthlessly stalked and hunted down by the worst of the worst on this planet, that is if I don't get him first."

"But Kevin—"

"I need the latest Trojan virus you're working on," Kevin said. He knew Wayne would have something in the works that would help him lay the trap he needed to set to take down the massive global network operated by Steelie.

Wayne spun around and stared at his Stanford Computer Science degree, "Jesus, you M.I.T.'s are stubborn."

"Well Stanford," Kevin said, "can you help me?'

Wayne shook his head, "Is that really an M.I.T. asking a Stanford for help?"

"Well?" Kevin said. There was a moment of silence. Kevin knew Wayne would concede; he had always been there for him.

"X-tractor," Wayne said, "we think it's Russian."

"Russian—even more perfect," Kevin said. "What's it do?"

"It attaches to emails—when they're opened it buries itself in the user's hard drive," Wayne said.

"That's it?" Kevin said. He needed something more to do what he had in mind.

"Nope," Wayne said. "It does the same thing with smartphones."

"Getting warmer," Kevin said.

"They'll spill their computer guts," Wayne said.

"Now we're talking," Kevin said. "And," he added prompting Wayne for more.

Wayne waited for Kevin's next prompt.

"Give me the big finish, Wayne," Kevin said. "Show me the money."

"At a preset time," Wayne said, "X-tractor starts sending the contents of the smartphone or computer to whomever you tell it to—all their emails, voice and text messages and contact information."

"I like that. Bait, auto hack, extract and disseminate," Kevin said.

"I've isolated it in the lab—I'll make it accessible for you," Wayne said.

"Time to go phishing and destroy some digital RATS," Kevin replied.

"And Kevin," Wayne said, "NIPC's got the encryption code—Matt said thanks."

Wayne looked at a picture of him with Kevin—deep-sea fishing. He smiled.

"Go get'em, Kevin," Wayne said.

Wayne started to hang up and then paused. He waited for Kevin to hang up at his end.

"I'll find a way to contact you," he said. "In the meantime, don't believe any reports you hear about me."

"I won't," Wayne said.

* * * * *

Kevin was determined he would not go to another AA meeting of the group he had joined. He did not want to listen to Meg grovel or try to explain away what she was up to. This meant he would not be able to find another AA meeting attendee trying to save himself and make amends by turning over a gun to him.

The next morning, Kevin exited a pawnshop carrying a pistol case and sprinted to his rental car. If his plan worked, he would be face-to-face with Julia's killer, and this time he would be prepared to finish the job.

CHAPTER 20

THE ROOM TEMPERATURE in Attorney General Waters' office was set to make icicles.

If emotional temperature were measurable, the mercury in the thermometer would have blown the glass bulb apart. This was on a scale like nothing Meg had ever seen or experienced before.

Meg sat at one end of a long table with the Attorney General at the opposite end. It felt like she was actually standing on top of a volcano. Special Investigators Palmer and Burgess sat just over halfway down the table, closer to the Attorney General. While they may have felt sitting further away from Meg was a sign she was off side with them, Meg figured they probably wished they had sat with her.

They were all waiting for a simmering Attorney General to erupt as he stared down at Joe Martelli from a raised high-backed leather chair. Joe sat next to the Attorney General—flush red from the simmering volcano.

It was about time, Meg thought, given the briefing just delivered to the Attorney General. For the first time, Attorney General Waters was getting the straight goods—an unfiltered version about what had been going on under his watch. Then she saw it in Waters' eyes. The lava was about to explode.

"I assured the President that the Witness Protection Program is bulletproof," Waters said. "I'm asking for more money to expand the program. And all the while, you're telling me we're on top of a little security problem."

Meg watched Joe wilt into his chair like a shriveled penis. It was good to see one of the boys finally get what they deserved.

"Isn't this a fine mess?" Waters continued.

"Sir," Palmer said, "we believe we've got the problem under control."

Meg saw the dirty look the Attorney General flashed at Palmer. It was a bad time to speak. None of the boys were safe right now.

"I lobbied the President," Waters said. "Told him other departments in his Administration needed to get their computer security in order. And all the while our own staff are picking us blind."

"Jensen and Murray are behind bars," Burgess said.

Waters stood and the volcano exploded, "In a few hours, I'm briefing the National Security Council on the NIPC initiative." He glanced at a photo of him and the President in happier times. "I will be defending the President's initiative; how it's reduced threats to national security, strengthened the security of public infrastructure and of our entire government's computer network—meanwhile, we have a nut in cyberspace."

Meg watched Waters' eyes. They turned to fire as he looked around the table.

"A nut who's amassing information on critical infrastructure assets," Waters said as his eyes landed on Joe. "Now I've got to tell them I've got a problem with the security of *my* own computer systems, the systems intended to uphold and safeguard the country's justice system. God-damn it— the Witness Protection Program to boot!"

"We've got an operative on the inside," Joe said. He tried to look past Waters' glare, "He's one of the best computer security people in the world."

Meg could no longer let this A-hole continue and jumped to her feet, "No! You've got a man who's lost his wife and unborn son. And now he's on the verge of being killed."

"What the hell is this all about?" Waters said.

"You said 'I don't care how we do it, but we need to get some new eyes on these cases—catch those bastards at their own game.' Well," Joe said, "Kevin Albright's the best, and he's working at Logic Computer Services."

"We suspect they're a major player in all of this," Palmer said.

Meg could tell that the Attorney General was ready to throttle Joe, and it could not come soon enough.

"You've really done it this time," Waters said. He motioned everyone to get out of his office.

Everyone, except Joe, stood eager to leave.

"Keep a lid on this until I can find the right time to brief the President," Waters said. "Now, get the hell out of here!"

Meg looked at Joe; he was still seated. *You stupid, stupid idiot*, she thought. Your career is over. She tried to suppress the other thoughts of the old boys club and the fact that those in power or fighting for power seemed to always have an Ace card they held back—just in case. She hoped that Joe did not have such a card on Waters.

Waters slowly turned to Joe, "Martelli, that means you too."

* * * * *

Kevin looked at his watch. It was after 10 p.m. Paul had sent the entire LCS nightshift staff home, except for Kevin. What Paul did not know was that Kevin knew what was going down. Paul had directed him to conduct an orderly shut down all the servers and not to leave before he returned. He had slipped into Paul's office at the very first opportunity this time and searched his file cabinets. He only had time to locate the street address for International Antiques and sent it to Wayne, in case he did not make it through the night.

Kevin's fingers kicked into a gear higher than overdrive, and were a blur as they flew across the keyboard. He needed to work quickly to get the X-tractor Trojan virus penetrating the computers of everyone affiliated with Logic Computer Services. He was convinced all those who signed up in the last few months did so in order to do business with International Antiques. It was highly unlikely LCS had signed on new clients who were not affiliated somehow with International Antiques. Who in their right business mind would sign on with an ISP on the verge of bankruptcy? The quickest way was to use the master list used by LCS to tell clients about scheduled maintenance and program updates.

He paused to read the email he was about to send out, "To LCS Master Client List; Code Update File Name X-tractor." He hit ENTER, the message instantly went around the globe to all LCS clients. This was the power of technology, a global reach—Russia, China, Iraq, Central and South

America, Canada, the United States—from anywhere in the world using wireless communications, in under a second.

Now, just like the deep-sea fishing he enjoyed with Wayne, he just needed to sit back and wait for someone to take the bait. Like watching the tip of a fishing rod, he watched the cursor pulse on the computer monitor. However, unlike the sense of anticipation he once experienced when he fished and waited for the big one to bite his hook, as time passed by without even a nibble, the waiting brought anxiety. Kevin needed them to bite. Swimming by the bait was not an option.

Then he heard a beep. He had a strike. A message appeared on his computer screen, "email opened by Hazze."

He smiled; he just landed his first big fish. He grabbed the telephone as his computer sounded a rapid series of beeps. He had just netted a whole school of big fish. He looked at the monitor and saw a succession of emails opened and acknowledgments flash up. *All right*, Kevin thought, *X-tractor do your thing.*

He dialed a number and listened to it ring. He was initially surprised, as someone picked up on the first ring. Then he realized that Wayne must have gotten through.

"Attorney General Waters.," a voice said over the phone.

"My name is Kevin Albright," Kevin said. "You might know me as Josh Burke. I'm in *your* Witness Protection Program. At the moment, I am taking care of some of your business for you."

"I've just—" Waters started to say.

"You have a major cyber conspiracy occurring on your watch," Kevin said.

"Mr.—" Waters was stopped before he could even get Kevin's last name out of his mouth.

"Mr. Attorney General, I'd like to chat," Kevin said, "but you've got a lot a work to do—starting with Martelli."

* * * * *

Waters still had the phone glued to his ear as he stood. There was a quick knock. Joe opened the door and started to walk in.

In one quick breath, Waters said, "Out, Martelli!"

Joe froze.

"You're done!" Waters said.

Joe immediately stepped back and closed the door.

"OK, Mr. Burke," Waters said, "or would you prefer I call you Mr. Albright?"

"Just do your job. I've just sent a little program to a few people," Kevin said. "Your NIPC people can expect some email."

Waters fell into his chair.

"In the meantime, get a team to International Antiques. You've got the street address from Wayne Helmes," Kevin said.

"Yes," Waters said.

"You've got ten-fifteen minutes, tops—to get the hackers who breached national security."

"OK, Mr. Burke. Listen I'm—" Waters said.

"I've got to go," Kevin said.

The receiver slammed in Waters' ear. All he could hear was the dial tone of a dead phone line.

* * * * *

An FBI car jumped the curb in front of a fortified office tower, and screeched to a stop just short of hitting a huge sign anchored in "FORT KNOX DEVELOPMENTS – Secure Offices Guaranteed."

Special Agent Larson had taken charge of the night raid. He jumped out of the passenger seat and motioned Special Agent Wells to the front door.

A black unmarked car screeched up beside them, flattening a temporary sign "Office Space for Immediate Lease." Special Investigator's Palmer and Burgess jumped out to join a swarm of government agents behind a battering ram, as it gathered speed and bashed through the front doors.

* * * * *

Larson was the first into the International Antiques offices. They were totally cleaned out. Wires hung from the wall outlets. Larson could not believe it; somehow, they knew a raid was going to happen.

Wells entered and surveyed the barren space.

Larson motioned Wells toward Big D's office.

Wells kicked in the door; the office was empty.

Larson rushed to the hacker's office and burst in. It was desolate—abandoned except for one computer and a monitor on the floor. Larson rushed up to the monitor and watched a stream of zeros and ones blast across the screen. *Damn it,* he thought, *they're scrubbing the hard drives.* They could have removed and taken all the hard drives, but they purposefully left one—to further piss off the authorities.

The monitor went black.

A flashing cursor appeared.

Larson watched the cursor pulse. It was too late to unplug the computer. It was already loaded and he knew what was coming next, and it was not good.

A message flashed up on the screen, "Contents Totally Destroyed!"

It's what Larson had expected would happen. Then the cursor pulsed again and another stream of characters blasted out on the screen, "Have a nice day," followed by a "smiley face" symbol. Larson lost it. They were good and arrogant beyond anything he had ever thought was possible. This was the new world of law enforcement—the world he would have to face everyday. Gone were the days of watching a security camera and catching criminals on video. They were now operating under the radar and totally invisible.

Larson's frustration turned to disgust as he looked around the room—he needed to unload or explode. He unleashed a kick, sending the keyboard crashing into the computer.

* * * * *

James stood at his office window staring into the blackness of night. His chest felt tight as he listened on the phone.

"We recovered a computer," Larson said.

"What about the data?" Waters said.

"Memory's wiped clean," Larson replied.

"What about using data recovery software?" Waters asked.

"They scrubbed the drives, might as well have dropped them into sulfuric acid," Larson replied.

Matt barged into James' office, "Our Moscow Desk intercepted a Kazakhstan transmission—they're scrambling fighter jets. Something's going down tonight."

James' stomach churned as if an ulcer was about to erupt. The President's words reverberated in his head, *We've got major targets—over a hundred million American citizens live in east-coast states. Hell, New York City alone is a nine-thousand square mile target, fifty million citizens!* His efforts at NIPC were failing terribly. His prayers had gone unanswered and a feeling of helplessness hit him like a nuclear bomb.

"Jesus Christ almighty," James said, slowly enunciating each word. "This could be the end!" He slammed the phone down.

CHAPTER 21

UNDER THE COVER of darkness, Steelie marched to the rear door of Logic Computer Services. He had no doubt about Big D's orders and was a man on a mission. His plan would be similar to Central America ISP jobs. He would permanently terminate LCS and that meant the total destruction of physical assets.

Just like the Central American ISP jobs, time was of the essence. The Internet Service Provider had become a major liability and Big D had made it clear to Steelie that he had to take care of LCS immediately—before the FBI raided the place. He would not be able to pull all the hard drives with the tight timelines and the crew he had.

Tonight, he was going with the alternative—explosives. It would be messy, but the FBI would have little evidence to pick through, just tiny pieces of brick, mortar, equipment and millimeter sized pieces of hard drives. If anything survived the explosion, the heat of the fire would ensure that nothing that was computer readable would be recoverable or readable. It meant they would have to start over using good old paper records and a couple of hard drives from Paul's office. It was standard practice—no off site computer backups were ever made. The information was too sensitive and it was just too dangerous.

Then he needed to find and kill Kevin Albright. The guy had become a bigger problem than the worst drug dealer he had dealt with. He had become a major threat to the good life he now enjoyed in the good old United States of America. He had come a long way since the police busted into his family home in Central America and killed his parents.

Steelie rang the rear security doorbell that would bring Paul, the night manager—come twenty-four seven LCS manager, to the back door. He could have had Hazze make up an electronic card to get in, but he needed to see Paul personally to deliver a message.

Paul opened the door immediately. Big D had called ahead and Paul had obviously been waiting for Steelie to arrive.

Poor bastard, Steelie thought. He did not have a clue about what was coming. The thought only lasted a millisecond. Paul's life was just the cost of doing business. Before Paul could speak, Steelie snapped his neck. He could have let one of the new thugs he was training do it, but nothing on this mission—absolutely nothing could go wrong tonight. Then he motioned to his new crew to join him. He had nicknamed them Linebacker and Wrestler.

Linebacker walked up with a duffel bag and handed it to Steelie. Wrestler followed closely behind.

Steelie motioned to his new thugs in training.

"Time to start proving you got what it takes to work for us," Steelie said. He pointed at Paul's body. "Get him away from the door," he said, and motioned toward a closet. "Throw him in there."

As the thugs dragged Paul to a closet, Steelie swung the duffel bag over his shoulder and headed down the hall.

* * * * *

Steelie entered the LCS Data Center. It was large and sterile looking. A heavy metal door swooshed, as it closed behind him, to seal the room. He immediately started to place explosives in the raised floor under the huge computer servers. His experience with ISPs taught him this was the brains of the operation. Destroy the brain, the body dies. Blow up the servers, there was no brain or memory for the FBI or other law enforcement agencies to recover.

* * * * *

Moments later, Linebacker and Wrestler arrived and rushed toward Steelie for their orders.

Steelie tossed a bag to Wrestler. "Keep putting the explosives under those computer servers," he said as he pointed to one side of the room. He turned to Linebacker, "Help Wrestler with the explosives. I'm going to get the files."

Steelie headed for the door to the office area. The explosion might destroy everything, but he needed the hard drives maintained in Paul's office. They contained all the current technical computer details about International Antiques' client profiles. The profiles were essential to re-establish the client accounts at a new ISP. Even more critical were the International Antiques working files maintained off-line in paper format by LCS—client names, phone numbers, emergency contacts, even backup passwords. This was the offline backup plan to get things back online.

A standing agreement with clients was International Antiques would never put a client's *personal* information into computer memory—someone could steal. After all, that was the very business Big D and Steelie were in—stealing computer secrets for their clients. They would all sink if the FBI got the profiles.

This had never happened to date. It was always something that got Steelie's adrenaline flowing. The thought about beating the FBI, or any law enforcement agency again, at their game, always did that. They would continue to pay for what was done to his parents.

* * * * *

Steelie stepped lightly as he entered the office area. He stopped and listened for the sound of staff working. If Paul had followed Big D's orders, he would have sent the nightshift staff home early. The silence suggested that Paul had followed orders. Then Steelie heard pages being flipped. He crept toward the sound and stepped up on a desk. Steelie could see Kevin sitting in his office cubicle at his computer, flipping through printouts. Tonight was working out better then he could have hoped. He stepped down off the desk, checked his Heckler Compact gun and approached Kevin in stealth mode.

* * * * *

Kevin stiffened. The hairs on the back of his neck were tingling again. This time, he sensed a presence behind

174 | DEADLY INVISIBLE ENEMIES: BOOK 2

him. It was either Paul returning to make sure he had finished shutting down the computer servers, or if he was really lucky, the International Antiques crew had arrived to terminate their relationship with LCS. If it was International Antiques, he hoped it was Steelie. He was ready this time.

"Well, well, well, Mr. Albright," Steelie said as he stopped two feet behind Kevin. "This is working out even better than I had planned."

Kevin whirled around. He was wearing a white shirt, the shirt stained with Julia's blood. It was a uniform. This was the blond thug that killed Jewels. Kevin was ready; he had a Glock 37 in his hand. He saw Steelie's surprised look.

"What took you so long?" Kevin said as he jumped to his feet.

Before Kevin could draw a bead with his Glock, Steelie grabbed the gun out his hand and pushed him back into his chair.

Steelie tossed the Glock across the room and pulled out his Heckler Compact.

Kevin's heart pounded like a hammer against his chest, as he watched a wicked ear-to-ear grin appear on Steelie's face. This was the fucking thug who had killed Julia. He knew Julia hated the word "fuck," but now it was so very appropriate.

"Your worst nightmare is nearly over," Steelie said. "And," he held up his gun, "while I'd like to chat—"

"You *fucking* son of a bitch!" Kevin said, as he lunged for Steelie.

"Temper, temper, Mr. Albright," Steelie said pushing him back into the chair. "Or should I say Mr. Burke?"

"Fuck you!" Kevin said.

"Now, Mr. Albright," Steelie said. "That's not very polite."

Kevin's emotions boiled over as his eyes scanned the room. What was he thinking? He had hesitated. He should have pulled the trigger as soon as he spun around. He had waiting to deliver a verbal message and watch Steelie squirm. He needed to calm down. Breathe and think, Kevin. He knew he had to get this bastard. He couldn't let him walk out of there. He needed to get his finger on a trigger and pull it—quickly.

* * * * *

Meg drove into the parking lot behind the Logic Computer Services office. She noticed a rental car in the parking lot. It looked a lot like the one Kevin had driven recently. She went to the rear door at LCS and tried it—it was unlocked. She drew her gun—a .500 Magnum. She had turned in her government issued gun. The Magnum was her father's gun. Until tonight, she had only taken it out of her closet to clean it and put in back into storage. She cautiously entered the LCS building.

As Meg slowly walked down the hallway, she spotted the thugs Linebacker and Wrestler through the glass window portion of the data center walls. The wall that surrounded the data center was finished with finished drywall on the lower portion and glass on the top half.

It looked like they were planting explosives in the data center. She needed to find Kevin, and then they would come back and take care of these fucking assholes. She wasn't a man, but one thing she was increasingly beginning to like was the language men used to describe people they hated. In this case, it fit these thugs.

She crouched down below the windowed portion of the wall and crept past the data center. There were two ways to enter the office area—one route was straight through the maze of screened offices. The other used the buffer corridor that enveloped the office area. In addition to serving as a firewall, the cement blocks also hid what was happening behind the wall. Meg chose the buffer corridor. It would get her close to Kevin's desk without detection.

* * * * *

Kevin's eyes narrowed as he watched Steelie pull a chain out from inside his shirt. Something dangled off it, but he could not make it out right away. He was burning up on the inside.

Steelie moved closer and held the chain in Kevin's face.

Kevin recognized the rings immediately. This lowlife had stolen Julia's rings. The rings he had given to Julia as a pledge of his love for all eternity were hanging off a chain around Steelie's neck. This is why the nurse could not locate the rings. This was probably why a grieving woman could not even hold her dead husband's rings in her hand as she tried to get closure.

Kevin fought to stand, but Steelie pushed him back into his chair.

"A little reminder that I had some unfinished business," Steelie said. "Wonder what your wife would say now?"

Kevin knew that Steelie was relishing every second of this. He fought with everything he had to stand, but Steelie pushed back harder.

"International Antiques, witness protection files, encryption codes," Steelie said. "We have been busy, haven't we? Too bad that you won't be able to put that information to use."

"I wouldn't be too sure about that," Kevin said.

Steelie cocked his Heckler Compact gun and raised it.

Kevin did not blink, as he watched Steelie aim his gun at him. He was not going to give a thug any more satisfaction than he already seemed to be enjoying in the moment. When he pulled the trigger, he would not be able to enjoy the moment where his victim squirmed and begged for mercy.

Meg burst around the corner from behind the cement buffer wall; her .500 Magnum pointed directly at Steelie's head. "Drop your gun!" she said.

Steelie looked at Meg. He appeared unfazed. "Look, Mr. Albright," he said. "It's your friend—Miss Justice Department."

Meg approached Steelie, her eyes and gun fixed squarely on him. "You all right, Kevin?" she asked.

"Getting better all the time," Kevin said. He pointed at Steelie, "This is the gutless excuse for a human being that killed my wife."

Meg motioned to Steelie with her gun, "I said drop your gun!"

"Come and get it," Steelie said.

"Drop it," Meg said. "Now!"

Steelie appeared to respond to her command, and then he hesitated.

"Give me a reason," Meg said. "You'll die now."

"OK," Steelie said as he dropped his arm, "all right." He bent down, "I'm putting it down. Don't get trigger happy."

In a flash, Steelie knocked Meg's .500 Magnum out of her hand and sent her flying into the corner. She bounced off a screen partition and hit the cement block wall.

Kevin jumped Steelie and knocked his gun to the floor.

Steelie slugged Kevin sending him to the floor.

Kevin caught Meg out of the corner of his eye. She was not moving. He turned back to Steelie who was now standing over him.

Steelie glanced over at Meg. His evil smile appeared.

Just then, Kevin unleashed a kick to Steelie's groin with such force it surely was for Julia.

Steelie doubled over and started to wilt.

Kevin jumped to his feet and delivered an uppercut that sent Steelie into an upright position. Before Steelie could take a breath, Kevin delivered another blow right between the eyes.

Steelie dropped like an anvil to the floor.

Kevin turned to Meg. Her eyes opened.

Steelie's anger kicked into overdrive. He reached for his Heckler Compact.

"Kevin he's—" Meg said.

Kevin spun and spotted Meg's .500 Magnum.

Steelie grabbed his Heckler Compact and fired as Kevin lunged for Meg's .500 Magnum.

Kevin was nicked in the left arm. In one quick motion, Kevin snapped up the .500 Magnum, spun and fired. He hit Steelie in the chest. Steelie's body chased the blood exiting his wound and smashed into the cement blocks behind the spatters of his blood as it splashed against the wall.

"That's for Julia," he said.

With a look of disbelief in his eyes, Steelie tried to raise his gun.

Kevin fired again.

"That's for my son," he said.

Steelie slid down the cement blocks, layer by layer and fell over, on top of Meg.

Kevin stood and caught his breath. He slowly walked over to Steelie's limp body.

He bent over, wrapped his fingers around Julia's rings and tightened his grip. He yanked the rings off with such a force that he nearly severed Steelie's head from his shoulders.

The chain burst into a thousand pieces.

Kevin turned away from Steelie—he could not stand the sight of this poor excuse for a human being. He could not look at him and think about Julia at the same time.

Kevin stared at the rings. *I got your rings back,* he thought and spoke aloud for the world to hear, "I got him Julia."

CHAPTER 22

KEVIN FELT A sense of relief; he had accomplished what he promised Julia he would do. But he had little time to think about it as he heard someone grunting. He gripped his gun handle hard and spun around.

It was Meg; she was trying to push Steelie's dead weight body off her.

Kevin dropped his gun and grabbed Steelie's body. He tossed it aside, like a bamboo mannequin, and extended his hand to Meg.

"You OK?" he asked.

Meg shook her head that she was OK as she reached for Kevin's hand. She suddenly stopped when she noticed Kevin's arm. "You're bleeding," she said.

Kevin looked at the wound on his arm and said, "Never noticed." Then he stared at Steelie. For a moment, he still could not believe Julia's killer was dead. He would never know why Steelie had murdered his family. He walked over to Steelie and kicked his foot. He did not respond. He still could not believe it. He checked for a pulse. He was dead, finally.

"We've got to get out of here," Meg said as she stood.

Kevin glanced at his arm, and then back at the computer he had been working at.

"In a minute—I've got one more thing to do." He ran back to the computer and studied the monitor. The email he was about to send before Steelie had interrupted him still stared back at him on his monitor. He read it one last time, "To iman@InternationalAntiques. Pipe Cleaner Contractor Address Update File Name X-tractor." This was the last important piece to closing off business. *If the I Man opened the email, the rest would be history*, he thought. He had modified the package specifically for the I Man. In addition to extracting and disseminating computer contents, he added computer program code to destroy both the data and program applications needed to read the information residing on the computer. A digital RAT relied on the programs that controlled network switches for electrical grids and pipelines. Without the computer program, the digital RAT could not access the switches. The power grids could not be shut down and pipeline valves could not be tampered with. It was a temporary fix, but it would get the job done. That was the genius of his plan. Even with all the firewalls and all the electronic defenses, it always came down to the human element. Kevin was betting the I Man would not only open the email, but he would also send it on to his clients and contractors, ultimately delivering the digital blow.

He punched the ENTER key. The cursor pulsed, and then the screen flashed back, "Message sent."

"We've got to get out of here," Meg said.

Kevin's eyes remained glued to his computer screen.

"In a minute," he said.

"Kevin, now," Meg yelled.

Kevin's computer beeped and the monitor flashed, "email opened."

"OK." He grabbed his Glock 37 and turned to Meg, "I thought you resigned."

Meg waved her .500 Magnum, "And let the boys have all the fun?"

Kevin shook his head, "Took a lotta guts."

Meg glanced at Kevin's crotch, "Don't you mean balls?" she said.

Kevin nodded; he deserved that payback.

Meg looked at Steelie, "Although it looks like you really didn't need the help," she said.

"Let's get out of here," Kevin said.

Kevin and Meg ran a neck and neck sprint down the hallway. Then Kevin stepped in front of her and burst through a door.

Meg followed.

Kevin realized they had surprised the thugs, who immediately dropped their explosives and reached for their guns.

Meg dove for cover under a table and Kevin followed her.

Shots rang out and lead ricocheted everywhere.

Kevin scanned the data center walls and ceiling for the data center's fire-suppression system detectors. He hoped this old deadly fire suppression system still worked. The thugs would die if it did, and there would be an evidence trail for NIPC. It also meant he and Meg had less than thirty seconds to get out of the data center or they would suffocate, as the system sucked all the oxygen out of the room.

Kevin pointed at the ceiling, "See those fire detectors?"

"What about them?" Meg said.

"They're toast," Kevin said. "As soon as we trigger the fire detectors, halon gas will be released and the room will seal automatically."

She looked at Kevin with a puzzled, *what the hell did that mean?*, look.

"The gas virtually sucks the oxygen out of the room," Kevin said.

Meg pointed her .500 Magnum at a timer and explosives hidden under a desk across from their hiding spot.

"See that?" she said.

The timer countdown was at 00:00:30 seconds.

Kevin glanced at the timer.

She saw his eyes widen.

"Holy shit!" Kevin said. Before Meg could respond, Kevin grabbed her hand and pulled her to the door, as bullets ricocheted around them. He turned and aimed his Glock at a fire detector.

Meg forced the door open.

Kevin kept pulling the trigger on his Glock until the clip was empty and the alarm bells started to ring as they escaped through the door.

The door swooshed shut behind them sealing the room.

Meg turned back to see the Linebacker thug run to the door and frantically try to open it. He couldn't. He started pounding on the door.

* * * * *

Big D watched from down the street, as a series of explosions turned the LCS building into hell's inferno. He had talked with Paul earlier that night and knew Albright was at work. He had ordered Paul to keep him there until Steelie arrived to take care of business.

He had trusted Steelie in the past. But the last few assignments Steelie had left him feeling that he had to step in on this one. He also knew that after Steelie took care of LCS and Albright, he would have to eliminate Steelie. This one would be a bit tougher as he had grown to like Steelie. But business always trumped friendships. And now Steelie was just an associate, someone Big D used to conduct business.

He was relieved tonight. Not only did it look like it was a trip he did not have to make, but he also did not have to personally kill Steelie. He never contracted out the "hits" on his "personal" associates. One thing he knew for certain, LCS was out of play, for good.

In the meantime, it looked like destruction of the evidence trail was complete. Unfortunately, he had lost the paper records to restart his business. At the moment, he was not sure he even wanted to restart it. However, Big D knew he had felt this way before. In his drug dealing days and even in Central America when they blew up a computer company, time would tell. For now, all that remained was to complete his escape. He would contemplate whether he really wanted to stay in this business any longer later, a lot later. Had he made enough money to put it all behind him? Yes, but. The but lingered.

Unfortunately, the pull of the adrenalin rush from "beating the system," be it drug lords, or law enforcement agencies, always left him feeling twenty years younger. He knew one thing; he hated the thought of getting old.

CHAPTER 23

JAMES HOVERED OVER Matt's Main Ops desk. He was worried about the fate of hundreds, maybe thousands of people at home, asleep.

NIPC was being flooded with INTEL. Was it real or just digital propaganda? Were they, whomever they were, testing the United States' mettle? Would it be a suicide bomber, a missile, fighter jet or a digital attack on critical infrastructure? Was the intended target North America or a NATO outpost or the oil and gas fields in Iraq—fields with American companies and American citizens?

In attempting to connect the dots, it was becoming increasingly clear they were dealing with two separate events, but none of it had been independently verified.

On one front, NIPC discovered a plan to launch some sort of attack from Kazakhstan. It took a "dead government contractor," Kevin Albright, to intercept the new encryption code needed to decrypt the plan. However, NIPC failed to decrypt details of the plan in time to jam Kazakhstan's digital infrastructure. The plans appeared to emanate from the Middle East. But that was suspect as the communications had bounced from ISP to ISP to ISP, country-to-country, traveling around over the globe—supported by a publicly funded Internet, accessed by privately profiting ISPs.

Foreign fighter jets had scrambled and an attack was imminent. Worse yet, it appeared the jets were actually working prototypes of the SF-X14, based on a downed U.S. fighter jet and an undisclosed hack into the military aircraft manufacturer's computer records containing design details. The Chairman of the Joint Chiefs of Staff had his work cut out for him. All James could do was monitor cyber traffic and try to glean INTEL, which *might* indicate where the fighter jets might strike.

On another front and adding to the confusion and complexity was that in attempting to piece the digital INTEL together, NIPC had identified that an attack emanating from inside the United States was imminent. Its impact would extend beyond the U.S.

James believed it could be some sort of cyber attack—perhaps an attempt to take out power grids or banks or a nuclear facility. This was the very reason NIPC existed, to protect national infrastructure from cyber threats posed by terrorists or rogue operatives. The twenty-six nuclear facilities and banking system were immediate considerations and on high alert. Nuclear facilities were implementing emergency procedures. The banking system was readying "offsite" digital records and backup systems. All U.S. airports were placed on high alert. Surveillance on all international flights coming into the U.S. was increased.

Matt's phone rang. He snapped up the handset, "Matt Arnet."

James strained to hear the conversation, but he was at the mercy of his top NIPC agent, Matt, for any information.

Repeating what he had just heard Matt said, "A virus." Then he glanced up at James. "Trojan," he paused and waited for more information. Then said, "Backdoored."

"What!" James said, thirsty for information.

"X-tractor," Matt continued to repeat snippets of what he was hearing as he listened to the caller, and then said "Fighter jets."

James could not stand it. He was about to explode as his analytical mind was already racing five steps ahead. Would his grandchildren be OK? He had talked to his daughter that morning. And earlier in the evening he told his wife to make sure she was close to their granddaughter.

"Potential threats," Matt said. "Kazakhstan computer ops," Matt spun around in his chair. "All down!"

James wanted to believe it, but he needed some kind of confirmation. NIPC had failed to jam Kazakhstan's digital infrastructure, so how could this really be happening?

Matt looked at James, "Logic Computer Services—Josh Burke."

"Josh Burke?" James said.

"Kevin Albright," Matt added.

James tried to calm the thousand knives piercing his stomach walls.

Matt hung up.

"A Trojan horse virus Albright launched took out Kazakhstan communications," Matt said. "Radar, voice, the whole damn digital network and jammed up the onboard fighter jet computers, HUD instrument panels and all the computer sensors on the fighter jets. They would've been flying in the dark literally with no digital support to launch missiles, bombs or rockets."

James dropped into a chair and took a deep breath.

* * * * *

Big D sat in the back of the Reagan National Airport lounge enjoying his last Cuban cigar before boarding a flight. He watched Special Agents Larson and Wells enter and flash a photo of Steelie to the bartender. He smiled, as Hazze had already shared photos of these agents with him. They were potential candidates to replace Agents Jensen and Murray, when the time was right. All he needed to do was create the right conditions to turn them into willing associates. All computer systems had weaknesses—people, and all people had a price. It just takes a bit of time to discover what the price is—money was only one currency.

Big D's cell rang. He answered, "Dempster."

"It's taken care of," the caller said.

"Good. His political ambitions were clouding his judgment," Big D replied. "Let that be a lesson."

"Everything is in place to transition," the caller said.

"You'll hear from me when the time is right," Big D said.

Big D closed his cell and spun his chair around to watch another airplane taxi to a runway and take off, its lights disappearing into the darkness. As much as he loved antique weapons of war, he loved the idea of flying—he had long wanted to be a pilot like his father, but he just could not bring himself to fly a plane. It was not the fear of flying, but the fear of isolation—actually being alone—in an aircraft, 10,000 feet above the ground scared the hell out of him.

The thought of flying by himself to gain his pilot's license was the last frontier fear he had yet to face. Maybe in the end, he just did not trust himself, something he would never admit to anyone.

Hazze and Darkside entered the lounge and walked past Agents Wells and Larson as they exited. Hazze scanned the lounge and spotted Big D. He nudged Darkside and they sauntered over to meet him.

"So, it's all done?" Big D said.

"Brian Dempster is no more," Hazze said. He gave Big D the once over, "His hair was bit longer, blond, but—"

"He died in an explosion," Darkside said with a mischievous grin.

"The price of pissing me off!" Big D replied.

Hazze handed Big D an envelope, "The new ID—we did a fingerprint swap and ID transference, and created new passports, Canadian, Australian and EU—"

"EU," Big D said with a surprised look on his face.

"Yah," Hazze said puffing up his chest. "Sixteen more countries, a piece of cake—cloned a government issued certified chip used in their passports."

"Great," Big D said, as he slipped the package into his jacket pocket, "Guess that about wraps it for now. Shop's closed." Big D looked at Hazze with a twinkle in his eye, and then said, "For now! Take a holiday."

"What about you, Big D?" Hazze asked.

Big D's eyes seemed to drift to a faraway place. "Gonna go live on an island," he said.

Hazze glanced at Darkside, "Some interesting things happening in China. If you need to—"

"I'll find you," Big D said. He noticed Hazze's momentary uneasiness. *Good*, he thought, that's the way he liked it. These guys would remain loyal to him, if for no other reason than they knew he had a global reach that went beyond computer networks and they did not want to test it. He swiveled his chair around to watch another airplane takeoff.

Hazze forced a smile as he and Darkside stood and left the lounge.

* * * * *

James stared out his office window into the night sky. His eyes followed the lights of an aircraft on the horizon. He owed a great debt of gratitude to Kevin Albright. NIPC owed a debt of gratitude. The American people owed a debt of gratitude, but they would never know it because, unlike 9/11 or Pearl Harbor, it was invisible, like it never happened.

A quick hard knock and Matt entered James' office.

James spun his chair around.

Matt shook his head in disbelief.

"You won't believe this," he said, "but we're getting files from all over the globe—drug deals in Central America, the real details about those Middle East plans to launch an attack from Kazakhstan." Matt sat down and took a breath, "There was never a planned attack according to government officials from Kazakhstan and China. Kazakhstan is among the top ten countries in the world when it comes to proven oil reserves and China has been aggressively working with the Kazakhstan government to secure access to reserves. The fighter jets were participating in a joint Kazakhstan-Chinese military exercise. We suspect its part of a plan to increase surveillance of the growing oil and gas pipeline infrastructure from Kazakhstan to China. They also emphatically claim that information about prototype fighter jets scrambling and suddenly being forced to land was a fabrication by some rogue media hacker in search of a story. It was all some kind of grandiose cover."

"A cover!" James said.

"Decoys! Real mission was called 'Pipe Cleaner.' Target was a two-thousand mile pipeline network stretching from Fort McMurray Canada deep into the States," Matt said.

"But how?" James said.

"We're trying to figure that out," Matt said. "What we know for certain is more than ninety percent of the oil we get from Canada flows through the targeted pipeline network. More oil than we import from Iraq, Saudi Arabia, Venezuela, and Kuwait OPEC countries combined. I don't need to tell you the impact that turning off that tap would have on our country."

"It would kill our economy," James said as the reality of it slowly sank in. "First the refineries—"

"Line ups at the gas pumps—" Matt said.

"If there was gas—probably gas rationing," James added.

"Selling for double or triple the current price," Matt said.

The moment of savoring any sense of a victory was over. James' mind raced ahead. "Any leads?" he asked.

"We're hunting for the I Man," Matt said. "Damn Chinese rogue operative's gone off the grid."

"I don't know how Albright did it," James said,

Matt piped in, "He sent an email to this I Man guy. The guy who triggered all the decoys—"

"Digital propaganda," James said.

"Including the Kaz attack," Matt continued. "But after the I Man's computer contents were extracted, Albright's program sent onboard fighter jet computers into overdrive, causing their systems to crash—the jets were literally forced to land or crash."

"We're damn lucky he's alive," James said as he grabbed the telephone and dialed. While he waited for the call to be put through, he turned to Matt, "I need to alert the National Security Council, brief the President right away—he's been waiting for CIA INTEL, looks like NIPC's got the *real* INTEL on the energy issue."

Matt looked at James as he waited for the phone to be answered, "One day, we may not be so lucky," he said.

"I know," James said. "It was so much easier fighting with planes and bullets. At least we could see them—track them, and they were physically limited to a target. Now we've got invisible enemies fighting invisible wars—going global in nanoseconds. Push one button on a computer and you can take out twenty-six nuclear reactors in twenty-six locations in less than a second, and no one would see you coming." James took a deep breath, "That's what scares the hell out of me!"

* * * * *

Meg looked around the Oval Office of the President. The room was full of men, Attorney General Waters, NIPC Director James Bullock, the CIA Director, the Chairman of the Joint Chiefs of Staff and the President. They were all listening to a woman. She wondered if even this would have made her father proud. While it still hurt, it did not seem to matter quite as much now. She had stepped up to the plate and did her job, the job she loved because she made a difference. Not because she was breaking up an old boys club, not because she had tried to be the boy her father wanted—but because she was being true to the daughter he had.

She took a sip of water and continued her briefing, "The National Security Agency Cryptology Unit took the unusual step of deep cover as soon as we realized the government's encryption programs were compromised."

She watched the President slowly pan the room. It was obvious that everyone in the room was out of the loop, except for the President.

The President zeroed in on the Chairman, "Our entire system of national security hinges on communication," he said, "and it was on the verge of collapse. I spoke with Ms. Taylor's boss over at the N.S.A. But, I also needed a back up plan—"

Meg could see the Chairman was trying to hide his disgust at being played.

"The training mission," the Chairman said.

The President nodded as he turned to Meg, "Ms. Taylor and Kevin Albright helped us tear down a network that was growing in size and threat—a deadly virus invisibly starting to eat the body from the inside out. By hijacking the encryption program developed for our government, they were on the verge of inhabiting 'our brain.' Once in control of the brain they would have been running our country—then who knows? Maybe the world."

Meg looked at Attorney General Waters, the man charged with overseeing the National Infrastructure Protection Initiative. She knew he wanted to defend his turf, his actions. But the witness protection security breach would keep him busy fighting just to keep his job.

"We destroyed the program that was intended to turn a two-thousand mile pipeline into one big pipe bomb," James said. "Casualties and damage to infrastructure would have been enormous."

"Pearl Harbor would have paled in comparison to this pipe cleaner plot," the President said. "The lives lost—with 9/11, the financial crisis and Hurricanes Katrina and Sandy—our country would have been pushed to the brink of survival."

The President turned to the CIA Director, who immediately turned to Meg, "Are you sure Mr. Albright is dead?"

Meg knew the CIA Director was also in damage control mode, trying to deflect any accountability for failure. She glanced at the President. Only three people—the Director of the NSA—her boss, the President and Meg, knew the answer with certainty. She turned to the CIA Director, nodded yes.

"May he live in eternity," she said, "with his precious Julia."

CHAPTER 24

GIGANTIC RED CEDARS creaked as they swayed and wrung freshly placed raindrops from their leaves. A narrow road meandered through a forest to the Vancouver Island beach house. The house was small, rustic and self-sufficient, with solar panels and a micro-sized satellite dish.

It was tranquil and out of the way. Canadian law enforcement agencies had selected the beach house, completed a sweep and moved on. Steelie was dead. As far as the world was concerned, Kevin Albright and Josh Burke were dead. There was no reason to continue the heavy veil of manned security.

* * * * *

Inside the beach house, a news anchor spoke on a television located in a cozy living room. "At least three people were killed in an explosion last night," she said. "Unconfirmed reports indicate a Megan Taylor and Josh Burke, both employees of Logic Computer Services, were among the casualties. The Attorney General would not confirm that a Megan Taylor once worked for the Justice Department, citing privacy laws. In related news, the President continued to face a barrage of questions about the National Infrastructure Protection Initiative cost overruns."

* * * * *

Kevin stood in the darkened room, his eyes glued to the television. A fire crackled, its warmth pushing the dampness out of the room. Kevin's bandaged left arm hung out of a short-sleeved tee shirt. He was *dead again*, well at least according to the news.

He walked to a laptop computer and sat down. He reflected for a moment, and then his fingers slowly moved to the keyboard, and began typing. The series of keyboard clicks picked up speed, but were slower and less intense— more subdued than in the past, not because of Kevin's gunshot wound. Each keystroke had a moment of reflection embedded; it was the end of a long journey.

Kevin paused and studied the computer screen, "To waynehelmes; Forever a family, may they rest in peace." He turned back to the television.

"In other news today," the television news anchor said, "Attorney General Waters told reporters that an internal review of the Federal Witness Protection Program concluded that recent deaths of informants reported upon by the media were not attributable to the program. He stressed the program continues to be an essential part of our country's justice system."

Kevin stood up and walked to the television. He suddenly felt compelled to lecture the news anchor, "Right," he said, "corrupt FBI agents stole the information and handed it to criminals."

"However," the news anchor continued, "in support of the President's priority to modernize computer infrastructure he did note that funding was being reallocated to update an antiquated computer system supporting the program's administration."

Half measures, Kevin thought to himself. Firewalls could be strengthened and security measures toughened to prevent outsiders from "breaking in," and stealing information or seizing control of computer systems. However, there would always be problems. These were only technical fixes, made by humans.

The real problem always came back to people. There were people who make it their mission to find new ways to bypass firewalls and there were people who got careless in applying security measures. And there were people who would sell out when confronted with financial difficulties. But the worst of the worst were the people in positions of trust who knowingly helped "criminals" gain access to systems and information to advance their personal agendas. They were the most dangerous of all because they worked on the inside, behind the firewalls and security systems designed to keep outsiders from breaking in.

"The Attorney General announced that Joe Martelli, his Executive Assistant, has left," the news anchor continued. "We attempted to contact Mr. Martelli, but he has not returned our calls, and sources indicate he just seems to have vanished."

"You've got to be kidding," Kevin barked at the news anchor, as if he had an open microphone and direct line to the news anchor. It was the "system," Martelli should have gone to jail, but he was probably given the option to "get out of town" or be fired and charged for the crimes he committed. No doubt, the Attorney General's handlers wanted Martelli to run to avoid the embarrassment a trial would bring.

Kevin walked back to his computer.

"The Attorney General also introduced his new Executive Assistant," the news anchor said. A photo flashed up on the television. It was the man in the car, who helped Kevin the night Julia was shot. He had loaned Kevin his cell phone to call Wayne.

Kevin glanced back at the television. The photo of the man was already gone from the television screen.

"When pressed, the Attorney General again cited privacy laws and refused to discuss reasons for Joseph Martelli's sudden departure," the news anchor said.

Kevin turned back to his computer. There was a rapid series of keyboard clicks, and then he paused to study the screen, "HUMAN VIRUS ELIMINATED. JUST KEEPING THEM HONEST." He clicked his mouse on the "Send" icon. The laptop responded with "Message Sent." Kevin turned the laptop off and folded the computer top down.

"And now we go to the White House, where the President is addressing lingering questions about national security and the National Infrastructure Protection Center initiative," the news anchor said.

Kevin spun his chair around to watch the television broadcast.

* * * * *

The President stood at the podium in the White House and addressed the press, "My predecessors stood firm in the defense of our land, sea, air and space. I remain committed to their defense, but make no mistake there is a fifth domain of warfare looming in the shadows and I am even more committed to ensuring our nation's safety and security are not compromised in cyberspace. I can tell you that the very fact I am *not* here today talking about a catastrophic event that cost us tens, hundreds or thousands of innocent lives, is a testament to NIPC's success. That's a cost I will continue to fight for and invest in."

The President paused and glanced at James Bullock, "And on that note, effective immediately, James Bullock, the National Infrastructure Protection Center Agency Director will report directly to my office."

* * * * *

Maybe there is hope, Kevin thought as he watched the President.

He picked up a piece of jewelry from the table beside him. It was Julia's diamond ring. He could not retrieve the ring Mrs. Wilson wanted so badly, but he did get some justice. Someday, he would see her again and tell her what he had done face to face.

Kevin leaned back in his chair and stared at the sparkling diamond ring he had given his precious Jewels, a ring she got to wear for a few hours—a very short period of time. He knew she had given him the greatest gift a person could give—a lifetime. The time to heal, time to find meaning, time to forgive his father and time to feel true deep love.

He could have chosen to drink and squandered it away, "faked it until he *never* made it," but then it all would have been in vain. That was a simple truth.

He heard Julia's playful giggle play in his mind and mused that she had told him *the actions of others were meant to make you stronger, if you search for the true meaning.* He smiled to himself. Somehow, out of all he had been through, he had managed to stay sober and was finally starting to heal. Jewels would have been proud. *No,* he thought, *she would have said it was always his for the taking, if he really wanted it.* He smiled to himself. *Why couldn't he have just figured this out sooner?* He will ask himself that question for the rest of his life.

Sebastian charged into the living room with his newest chew toy—a wooden stick. Kevin snapped back into the moment. He stood and walked to a bag in the center of the room. He unzipped it and reached inside to pull out the last physical memory of Julia she had touched—the bloodied white shirt. He needed to let go of this *bad* memory and hang on to all the *good* memories they had created and shared.

He pulled back the fireplace spark guard and looked at the lipstick on the collar one last time. He inhaled one last smell of the scent of Julia's perfume. As the perfume filled his lungs, he tossed the shirt into the fire and watched the flames lap it up, like the devil devouring Steelie and freeing him of Steelie's hold on his life.

* * * * *

Sebastian started to bark and scratch at the beach house door.

"All right, Sebastian, all right," Kevin said. "We'll go down to the beach." He grabbed Sebastian's newly chewed fetching stick.

Sebastian barked again. Kevin froze. He had heard that bark before.

Before he could do anything, the door blew open.

It was Julia. He was sure she present with them.

His eyes welled up with tears.

* * * * *

Kevin and Sebastian walked on the deserted beach. Their silence spoke volumes to each other. What do you say when you have lived knowing your soul mate, your master, has died and then you feel the presence of your soul mate and master in the midst of the beauty created by God? Devine intervention, man made intervention—it really did not matter. They were together spiritually.

Sebastian jumped into the ocean and swam for a piece of driftwood.

Kevin's mind was still processing all that had happened—international criminals meeting with government agents, the theft of the United States Government encryption program and the threat to national security. Only the President, the National Security Agency Director and Meg knew the details—it was all on a need to know basis.

Kevin stopped and looked back behind them. All he saw was one set of fresh human footprints, and a trail of dog paw prints on the sand that disappeared into the ocean, and then reappeared, repeatedly.

He started to walk again. As he did, he watched Sebastian as he charged down the beach, chasing the waves as they receded and running from them as they advanced.

In the distance, a man walked toward him, his features were indistinguishable. Behind him, a single trail of footprints.

As they got closer to each other, Kevin reached behind his back and under his jacket. He wanted to make sure his Glock 37 was handy. Even though only a few people of the President's choosing knew where he was, it would be a long time before he would trust anyone or any situation as being totally safe.

Kevin could not be certain that International Antiques was larger than Steelie. But he was sure that some of his encounters with strangers would be with the people behind the faceless names that he had crossed paths with in cyberspace. He vowed to spend the rest of his life aggressively hunting down any new rogue "International Antiques" in cyberspace.

The man got closer to Kevin. It was not a man he had seen before.

As he got closer to man, Kevin felt his heart racing.

"Take it easy, Albright," he said to himself. "He's just an old man out for a walk on a deserted beach."

Kevin gave a friendly smile as he passed the man.

Big D smiled back.

Another huge wave crashed in.

Kevin turned to watch the wave retreat. The footprints left in the sand by Big D, Kevin and Sebastian had vanished—as if they had never been there.

Kevin knew he and Julia had vanished from the lives of their friends, but he had been given another chance to do it right.

It begged the question, what would soul mates give up to be together—everything?

What would soul mates do to stay together—anything?

Everything and anything was who Kevin believed he and Julia were, and he would do and feel everything and anything to honor Julia.

AUTHOR'S BIO

Story has always been a part of who Harold Lea Brown is—it is in his blood. In his teens, he told story through music when he played in a rock band. Later he told story through award winning poetry and used story as a way of communicating corporate history and vision as a chief business strategist. He has also published award winning technical articles in information management. His family roots are Norwegian and Finnish, where story is core to passing on history to future generations.

He has appeared as an extra or actor in more than fifteen Canadian, U.S. and international co-productions, commercials, industrial films; made-for–television movies and series, and feature films. He has studied the producer side of the film and television business, and received the Gerri Cook Memorial Award for the Most Promising Producer; and has worked as a contract producer. He believes that story is life well told.

Deadly Invisible Enemies: Hunt for Evil is Harold's second novel. To date, he has written seven award-winning feature length screenplays, garnering recognition at film festivals and screenwriting competitions in Canada, the United States and Mexico.

DEADLY INVISIBLE ENEMIES
EVIL RESURRECTION
Book 3

Secrets have deadly consequences, especially in a digital world.

In *Deadly Invisible Enemies: Evil Resurrection,* the real and virtual world, and Kevin's life, are in turmoil and unknown enemies are circling. Will deadly invisible enemies finish destroying Kevin? Can anyone cut the head of an evil cybercrime organization? Will Kevin uncover more secrets about Julia's death? Can he fight off his inner demons? Is an even more sinister plot underway on the Internet in cyberspace that could destroy countries and divide the world?

For more information about Harold and his creative endeavors go to:

www.storychaser.com